THE CHINA AFFAIR

J. T. GOOCH

ISBN 978-1-956696-31-8 (paperback)
ISBN 978-1-956696-32-5 (hardcover)
ISBN 978-1-956696-33-2 (digital)

Rushmore Press LLC
1 800 460 9188
www.rushmorepress.com

Printed in the United States of America

FOR

Lily
Jack
Meghan

CONTENTS

PREFACE

This story begins in China and ends in Chicago. Several twists and turns occur that cause readers to wonder just what the hell is happening next: the romance along the banks of the Xian River, the trial of an innocent female Chinese teacher, the smuggling of a Chinese woman OUT of China, a police "sting" operation in Chicago, the placing of a bomb in the Willis Tower, and, oh, yes, what happens to the bomb?

The first wisdom of this story is that "things are not always what they appear to be!" It is fiction; fantasy fuels the fiction to high levels of imagination. The author uses the story and the characters as vehicles to express certain viewpoints. History is full of such fictional comments; for example, if in the heat of battle, John Paul Jones did not say, "We have not yet begun to fight," he should have. If "Stovepipe Johnson," a partisan in the Confederate States Army, did not say when he occupied the hotel in Newburgh, Indiana, "Do not flicker an eye nor finger a trigger, we have you surrounded," he should have. History would be boring without such fictional assists.

The characters are composites of several individuals as one single person could not fit their descriptions.

The author disclaims any resemblance to real situations or real people.

"Beware of china! Beware of China!" The old man chanting this message was walking around the Beijing airport terminal banging on a long tube-like drum that resembled a round cardboard container for maps, and occasionally he would hit a little cymbal that he also carried with the drum. Such was the first encounter the American teachers had who were destined to experience China.

"What is he saying?" one of them asked.

"I don't have the foggiest," another responded, "but he is persistent."

The team leader who had traveled in China several times offered that "He is a typical old fart that hangs around public places and pan handles. Walk on, don't even look at them because if you do they sense that you are an easy mark."

The allure of the strange looking little man proved to be too much for the curiosity of a couple of team members, and they listened to his bewitching performance. The old man now turned on as he had an audience and began banging away, chanting, and doing a little jig.

"He really is wound up now," one of them said.

"Yeah, it would help if we knew what the hell he was saying," the other responded. A bystander who was waiting for a flight observed this scene, offered his expertise: "He is warning you about China."

"But, what is there to be warned about in China?" one American asked.

The bystander smiled, "That is why you must listen to the soothsayer. He is telling you China's secrets. He says, 'Beware of China, beware that China will blind your vision, China will play tricks on your mind, China will dazzle you with the beauty of its mountains, its rivers, beware of the beautiful China nights, they are seductive.'"

"Why is he telling us all these things?"

"He knows you are visitors and this is his way of telling you about his country and also, suppressing a laugh, his way of making a few extra bucks."

The old man went on and the bystander translated, "Beware the mysteries of China, beware the China surprises…"

"What the hell did I just tell you guys!" the team leader yelled. He broke the spell of the old man who glared at him when he sensed his audience was about to be rescued.

"I cannot take care of you if you do not listen to what I tell you!"

"What is the problem of listening to something like this?"

"The problem is these guys are pros at pan handling. You have never seen pan handlers and beggars until you have come to China! For example, look at that kid over there who is following those people. Look at his desperate, pleading face. Do you think that is normal? That kid is a pro."

"He looks retarded to me," another offered.

"Whatever! But, if you start running around like a bunch of cats, you are on your own!"

This was the first of many times that Micah (Mike) Nussbaum, team leader, tried to rein in the American teachers and to protect them from what he perceived as perils to the uninitiated travelers to China. He had been to China several times, had studied the language and culture, and headed up the teacher exchange program at Burkholt College in Peoria, Illinois. He prided himself on knowing his way around.

Mike then designated a place in the terminal by a fountain and an indoor tree to wait for the tour guide. The teachers piled their luggage into a small mountain of suitcases, carryon bags, and camera cases and waited for the tour guide and bus to take them to their Beijing hotel. Certain ones volunteered to watch the bags while others went to the restroom or sauntered around the waiting room. This became a familiar scene at all the other airports and hotels they would visit.

After some time, a Chinese man carrying a little green flag on the end of a flexible stick and a sign with "American Teachers" on it came through the front door. One of the Americans went to guide him to the pile of luggage and he asked for Micah. Mike had spotted him and was headed in his direction. "Let's load up, it is time to go," he barked. "Where is Tony?"

"He was here just a minute ago. Maybe he went to the restroom," someone volunteered.

"Well, go look for him. We need to get to the hotel."

Tony was wandering around the airport looking for photo opportunities. An architecture teacher, he constantly looked at building designs and construction techniques. He found many interesting examples in China. His family was from Arkansas but his father, tired of share cropping for the "white dudes", moved to Baltimore where Tony came into the world, and his parents named him Antonio for an Italian pizza place. This name plagued him most of his life.

"What's a black bro doing with a name like Antonio, Antonio?" Tony finally had the patent answer to these questions: "Call me Tony, Antonio, bro, black, African-American, or whatever the hell else you want but do not call me "late to supper!" So early in life he learned how to hold his own with jokesters.

"Tony, Mike says to load up."

"Right. Let's go."

The team loaded the bags and the bus made its way toward Beijing. The guide perched himself on top of a bag that was in one of the forward seats and said in perfect English, "My name is Eddie. I could tell you my Chinese name but you would not be able to pronounce it, and it would mean nothing to you. I will be your guide while you are in Beijing. If you have any questions please ask me. Today, you are tired after your long journey so we will go to the hotel, check in, and you will rest. Tomorrow morning, we leave the hotel at exactly 8:30am, not 8:31, not 8:35, but at 8:30am. Anybody not at the door at 8:30am will be left behind. Is that not right, Mike?"

"That is correct. We run a tight ship!"

As the group started the process of checking into the hotel a large crowd gathered in the front parking lot. In the middle of the crowd were the two American females of the team, two gorgeous creatures, one a blonde and the other a brunette. They had been college classmates and were using this trip to visit with each other and to catch up on old boyfriends, etc. Now they were enjoying their celebrity status in China for few Chinese had seen such beautiful American females this close.

The brunette was Tonya Lynn Burns and the blonde was Brooke Ashley Chambers. One was as pretty as the other.

When Mike saw what was going on the seethed, "Who is handling their luggage?"

"We brought it in."

"You should not have done that! They should be responsible for their own damn luggage! If someone else handles it for them they will never do it themselves."

After checking into their room and freshening up two of the team members ventured out to the busy pedestrian, bicycle, and motor scooter street in front of the hotel. Less than one block away on the corner was their first McDonald's experience. This McDonald's had free internet access.

They ordered Big Mac meals and caught up on news. Jack Thomas was from southern Indiana, a native-born Hoosier with an Indiana University education under his belt; Bradley Crawford was from eastern Kentucky, had graduated from the University of Kentucky, and had gotten a teaching job at Burkholt College. They taught together several years before Bradley changed jobs. Of the team members they probably were closest in friendship except possibly for the two females.

Bradley taught political science, "Well, the commies have not gotten us yet."

"No," Jack, the social historian, said, "but wait until we start the counterrevolutionary brainwashing we are going to do when we start teaching Mao's disciples and laughed."

"Yeah. I do not understand how they (meaning Chinese authorities) allowed us into their country, two American professors who are capitalists to the bone!"

Jack laughed, "Two capitalist running dogs. China will never be the same after we finish our work here. Mao will turn in his grave."

"Hell," Bradley added, "Mao will be on a rotisserie when he sees what we are doing."

They both laughed heartily at what they thought was their little private joke at Mao's expense.

Jack commented, "You know we are in Beijing and are eating the exact same damn "fast-food-nation" Big Mac we could get in our hometown! Wonder what Mao would think about that?"

"Who cares? I am going to enjoy this Big Mac, especially after that crap they had on the plane."

Suddenly Jack exploded, "Look at that car out there! It looks like my Le Sabre Buick," and after looking closer, he said, "It is a Buick; it has Le Sabre on the rear fender! Would you look at that, a Buick Le Sabre in Beijing?" (Mike later told him about the Beijing Buick factory.)

They finished eating during which time Jack commented about how well the people dressed, how they laughed and smiled, and how they seemed to be so happy. This optimistic moment was interrupted when they began a conversation with a physician from the Netherlands who had come to China to hold a seminar on open heart surgery. He, his wife, and two daughters landed on the coast and drove an automobile to Beijing.

They saw much of the countryside and saw hundreds of Chinese working in rice fields much the same way their ancestors had for thousands of years. The doctor concluded, "The new China has a way to go!"

After touring the usual places in Beijing such as Tiananmen Square and the Great Wall, the teachers prepared for their next destination, Xian, where the road for silk was famous. They walked the ancient walls of the city. After that they stayed in Guilin, a city famous for art and for their World War II activities to resist the Japanese. The Li River was next on the tour with fishing birds, bamboo, little limestone mountains, and the meandering river.

Finally, they reached Changsha Airport. Changsha was full of smoke as farmers burned their rice fields in spite of the law as traditions are very strong. The head of the English department welcomed them and took them to Changsha Education College, their teaching destination. They unloaded their luggage and settled into their rooms.

In addition to Thomas, Crawford, Calhoun, Mike and the two single females, there was a retired attorney, Frank Dennison, and a married couple, Dan and Mary Osborne. The group paired off to adjust to sleeping arrangements. Jack and Bradley shared a room as did the married couple, Tony and Frank, the two single females, and Mike had a room to himself. The rooms were on the first floor of the dormitory. Each had two beds, one wardrobe, a night table between the beds, and a single bathroom and shower. The toilet had western style fixtures; the shower had water running through an electric heater.

The rooms were comfortable and adequate. Meals were in the private dining room off the main student cafeteria. The cooks were eager to please the Americans and prepared special meals for them. One day there was a bowl of boiled eggs for breakfast as someone said Americans ate boiled eggs. Another time a big bowl of mashed potatoes appeared. Watermelons were available between classes as a snack to cool off in the hot summer in southern China.

There was a lot of experience in the group of American teachers. A political scientist, a social historian, a sociologist, an architect, a public relations person, a home health nurse, a math teacher, and a home life educator. Each teacher was to teach their subject to the Chinese English teachers in conversational English. The classes rotated from teacher to teacher so that students would get equal time with each teacher.

Teaching became structured after the first day. Classes changed when the head of the English department or someone else rang an old school bell. There would be a break in the teachers' lounge with fresh watermelons.

The lunch break was a longer time off as many students and teachers took time for a brief siesta to get through the heat of the day. Some students took naps in the classrooms, and teachers generally spent this time in their rooms. Then the afternoon classes resumed until the end of the day.

After the day was over class leaders had students to clean the rooms and to put things in order for the next day.

When teachers had finished the evening meal there was usually some plan to go somewhere. The college gave class leaders money to pay for the expenses to entertain the teachers. The group gathered around 7:00pm and started walking through the ancient streets of Changsha. The most popular place soon became the dancing area in the park along the Xiang. The people in charge fenced off an area, provided chairs, music, and hot tea. For one Yuan a person got music, hot tea, and all the dancing a person wanted.

The students wanted to dance with the teachers to talk and to learn more about the United States. It was during the dancing that Angela, one of the class leaders, stood out from the rest. The dancing stopped at 10:00pm and students and teachers walked together holding hands back to the college. There was a little grocery on the corner of the street to the college; it became standard procedure for Jack to buy everyone an ice cream bar of some kind. The owner of the store soon smiled when he saw the group approach.

When they got to the gate of the college, the gate keeper opened it for them and then locked it. He lived in a small room so he could open the gate anytime during the night. Then everybody went into the dormitory and a house mother locked the heavy wooden front door. Later Bradley took exception to the locked door! The college relented and left the front door unlocked.

Plans changed every night. One night the teachers went to the water show which featured music coordinated with water shooting into the air with different colors flashing. Another night was the night to eat at one of Changsha's restaurants. One night Bradley and Susan rode up on a bicycle he had just bought. He was excited about buying a bicycle for $20. Soon five teachers bought bicycles, loaned them to students, and generally rode them around the area. On a free day Bradley and Jack and some students rode the bicycles to Orange Island. The idea was to leave the bicycles with the students when the teaching session was over.

Susan was a student the previous year at Changsha Education College. She knew there would be other teachers coming from Bradley's school. Because of her the teachers felt very much at home for she was an excellent translator and guide.

Finally, the time to leave approached. The classes enacted skits in the auditorium about American life they had studied; for example, one class acted out a day at the beach, another class presented the typical American outdoor bar-b-cue. Other students performed on musical instruments. Then it was over, and the teachers were to leave the next morning.

The morning of departure many students came to say their farewells. Some cried; it was an emotional time. Bradley came into the teachers' lounge to tell Jack Angela was there to see him off. They said goodbye the night before when Jack gave her the bicycle but her brother came with a car to haul the bicycle home.

Jack ran out of the lounge to catch them leaving. The brother stopped the car, Angela got out, and gave Jack a hug and said, "These days at Changsha Education College have been the happiest in my life. I will miss you!"

Jack mumbled, "I will miss you too!"

Angela got back into the car, never looked back, and the car moved out of sight. Neither she nor Jack had any idea how their paths would cross again.

THE INCIDENT

The unfortunate retarded youth that slithered around the halls of the Changsha County Middle School was the headmaster's son. An accident at birth, he never had normal intelligence and was at a mental level slightly above a moron. The teachers who had him in classes knew his mother did his homework and that was the way he passed through school. His father's prominent position gave him privileges he would never have enjoyed otherwise. Unemployable, the school retained him as a general fixer-upper, and a gopher that gave him access to every classroom and office in the school. The faculty called him Junior. Junior reacted slowly to peoples' conversations, talked with a slur or lisp to his words, and his mouth hung open with a lower lip that curled downward that exposed his lower teeth. He had difficulty closing his mouth because his bite was off with protruding upper teeth. When he laughed the sound was like someone wheezing and trying to stifle a sneeze when they cannot quite do it and they are both blowing air out of their mouth and sucking air into their mouth at the same time. Junior slightly dragged one leg instead of picking it up totally off the floor. He entered classrooms when teachers worked by themselves and creeped in so quietly they would not hear him and suddenly they would see him standing there looking at them. Teachers agreed that he made their skin crawl but what could they do? He was the headmaster's son, and the headmaster was the absolute law in the school.

When the school hired Angela to teach English and political training, she noticed Junior as she unpacked teaching materials in her classroom. Junior eased himself into her classroom and watched her bend over, open the boxes, and lift the items onto shelves located along the wall of the room. She concentrated on emptying the boxes and did not know he was there until she heard this lisping sound that resembled the hiss of a snake, "Miss Angela." She whirled toward the frightening sound and confronted the creature that stood before her. "Yes," she said slowly, "I am Angela."

"I am Junior. The office sent me to help you move into your classroom" After her initial fright Angela appraised Junior and slowly concluded he appeared to be harmless, and she began to develop twinges of pity for him; however, when she told him she did not need his help he wheezed, "But, the office sent me here to help and I cannot go back to the office if I do not do anything." This show of resistance alarmed her but she thought she would have him bring some more boxes from the storage area.

"Thank you," he lisped and gave her his goofy smile, turned and started out of her office but stopped in the doorway, turned and looked directly toward her and said, "I like you!" After Angela finished moving materials into her classroom, the teacher in the next classroom came in and introduced herself and said, "I see you have met Junior." "Yes." "He is the headmaster's son and has the run of the school. He is creepy but he has never done anything that we know." Angela did not comment as she was new to the school and he was the headmaster's son. "I am happy to be here and to start my new job. I hope the other teachers are as nice as you have been," Angela commented. That was the end of the first day at Changsha County Middle School. Angela plunged into her work in the next few days. The school selected her from several people who competed for the job, and the headmaster advised her that this job was going to take a lot of work. She spent hours preparing for her public class that the headmaster and senior teachers observed. She knew they would dismiss her if she did not do well in the presentation. After the public class teachers congratulated her as teaching like an American. She handled the political training classes quite well for she had had extensive schooling on political philosophy. Political training prepared the students for military mandatory drill, learning how to march, and how to act as one unit. When the students went for military training, Angela took the class outdoors and presented it to the young cadet military officers who would put them through the routine. This was familiar to Angela for she remembered the same training.

When she returned to her classroom to prepare for other classes, she felt her hair tingle as though someone was watching her from shadows of empty rooms. She passed it off as normal jitters of being in an empty school while classes were on the drill field. But, often, Junior would take form in the doorway to her classroom and want to talk.

"Junior, I am busy. It is good to see you. Do you not have some work you need to do?"

"Not right now, Miss Angela," he drooled, "I do not have to do anything unless someone tells me to and nobody has told me so I am not working."

"But surely, you could clean some blackboards or sweep a floor somewhere? Carry out some trash!"

"All right, Miss Angela." He would give her his goofy grin and slowly move off into the halls of the school.

After being there for about two months, Angela commented to other teachers in the lounge about her suspicions of Junior. "Is it my imagination, or does his sexual member not swell when he comes into the classroom?"

The other teachers hooted and teased her. "What are you doing looking between his legs? Maybe you turn him on, and has he asked you for a date?"

After the tittering died down, Angela said, "In all seriousness, I do not believe he should be in a job where he is around young girls and female faculty for that matter. He is not to be trusted."

The teachers agreed with Angela's comments, but school went on as usual.

It was very hot in Changsha County Middle School. Without air conditioning, the classrooms would reach temperatures where it is not unusual to sweat through shirts and pants while teaching. Water bottles were everywhere. Ceiling fans stirred the air but provided on fleeting moments of comfort. Students hogged the fan space by huddling together in the middle of classrooms. The fans made a certain amount of squeaking noise so teaching would have to be loud enough to be heard above the fans. Fortunately, students did homework in school as home environments were not conducive to learning. This relieved teachers so they did not have to talk all the time.

Changsha County Middle School fulfilled the mission to educate the masses. The philosophy of education was to do everything to education and to train the new leaders. That included political training and military drill. Also, language study was mandatory; English was the most popular second language.

Angela was proud of her job and worked very hard. Her biggest problem was dealing with the class of spoiled brats that had entered the first level of middle school from the elementary. The headmaster suggested to her in the pre-job conference that she should "take charge" immediately of this class and let them know she did not tolerate disrespectful behavior. She did just that, and in the two-month performance review, the headmaster praised her success in handling the unruly class. He particularly complimented this group as it was an English class, and the students had made good progress.

The day after the two-month evaluation was a student activity day. Students participated in their favorite activities; many of Angela's students chose to have extra drill exercises. The job stress was reduced as she had proven her capability. She was anxious to write her American friend for she knew of his concern for her to tell him of her success.

Angela used the activity to her best advantage to make lesson plans. This always involved serious concentration and usually some research, and this was no exception. She became oblivious of the comings and goings of the students until she suddenly realized how quiet the school had become. For the first time that day, she checked the time, and she had stayed 35 minutes after school was dismissed.

She decided enough was enough and put her materials away, cleared her desk, and checked her watch again to see that it was now 45 minutes after school hours.

As she was making her way out of the classroom, she had an urge to use the bathroom. The bathrooms were at one end of the building separated from the classrooms by the stairs that gave access to the three floors of the school. When someone used the bathroom, the had to cross the stairs to get there. The administrative offices were at the opposite end of the building. Angela's room was in the middle of the second floor so she moved toward the end of the building to the bathroom.

She felt the emptiness of the campus and debated whether to endure the school bathroom for it was notorious for strong smells and for not always being clean or to wait until she reached her apartment.

She decided to use the bathroom. The little stall area was quiet as a tomb. She positioned herself over the floor fixture, gathered her long skirt above her waist, held it with her upper arms as she lowered her panties and then squatted on her flattened feet and relieved herself. She thought she heard a strange noise but then believed it must have been her water gurgling in the fixture. When two shoes appeared in front of the stall, her head and back tingled with fright and as she looked upward her face froze with fear. An addled-headed Junior was looking down at her. Her piercing scream jarred him into action as he fell down upon her and caused her head to bang against the wall and also to cause her to lie prostate on the grimy floor of the stall. The blow to her head stunned her as she felt her backsides slide into the smooth contours of the porcelain urinal. As she slid into the fixture it squeezed her thighs together.

Junior was struggling to get one hand between her legs to lift her out of the urinal and to spread her thighs so he could get at her female parts and with his other hand he was trying to get his belt loose and his pants undone so he could get his swollen maleness out of his pants and penetrate her.

Although groggy, the sensation of sliding into the fixture and the awful smell of Junior's breath exhaling through the wheezing of his mouth gave her enough consciousness to realize what was happening. She had the presence of mind to realize that her panties were gathered about her knees and she reached for them and tried to pull them up as Junior's hand was groping between her legs. He realized what she was doing and crammed his knee between her legs and pinched the tender insides of her thighs against the hard surface of the porcelain fixture. This sharp pain caused her to cry out and cleared her mind; her fear now changed to anger at what this moronic creature was trying to do to her.

She tried to push him off but he was too heavy and he had the advantage of being on top of her. She was also wedged in the porcelain urinal. By this time Junior had freed his male organ and as it assumed its threatening posture Angela knew she had to do something fast to break free. As she saw his threatening body part, she thought to herself, "You mental son-of-a-bitch if you want to get that thing inside me, I am going to help you!" She grabbed it with both hands and in a powerful sit-up motion pulled it into one side of her mouth so she could chomp down on it with her jaw teeth in a powerful bite.

Junior let out a blood-curdling wheezy yell, grabbed for his wounded body part, and rolled on his side in a fetal position and started whimpering with a lisping, wheezing sound. Angela bounded up, pulled her panties back on and ran out of the bathroom. She got on her bicycle and started toward her apartment. When she got home, she sat in the dark and shook.

After her nerves calmed, she took a long hot shower and let the water cleanse her mouth, her hair, and her body. She fell exhausted onto her bed and thought so strongly of her American friend and wondered if his heart would travel to visit her tonight. If it does, it will return with a troubled spirit. She fell asleep wondering whether her troubles were over or whether they were just beginning.

WOLFMAN

Jack perked up when he read the introduction to his e-mail: "Hello, Jack, you capitalist running dog. How are you? That could be only one person, "Wolfman!"

Wolfman was one of the older Chinese students who fancied himself as a ladies' man and kept trying to get the American female teachers into his new car. They avoided him, and the Chinese students passed him off as a joke. But, undeterred, Wolfman persisted and knew that sooner or later an unsuspecting female would succumb to his special charm.

Wolfman's message got Jack's attention! It was alarming and brief, "Jack, we need to talk. Let me know if you can chat at our usual time!"

Jack responded, "Hey, Wolfman, you communist pig, I am fine. Hope all is well with you! Let's talk at our usual time."

For some reason, Wolfman took Jack in as his long-lost buddy and they developed a relationship of laughing with each other and exchanging barbs with each other."

When they started their chat it was serious and all business. "What is going on?" was Jack's first comment."

"All hell is breaking loose here," Wolfman replied. The police are rounding up teachers connected to the college and teachers at the Changsha County Middle School, and there are rumors the national cultural director is in town. They are questioning the president of

Changsha Education College, the dean, the head of the English department, several students and even residents along the streets leading to the college."

"What the hell for?" Jack asked in disbelief.

"It seems your little sweetheart, Angela, is charged with subversive activities and anti-government sentiments in her teaching at Changsha County Middle School.

"What activities do they say he has been doing?"

"For starters, they allege fraternization with enemies of the state such as you. Further, they say she was unduly influenced with your capitalist ideology and has been spreading subversive ideas. They believe there is a major outbreak of anti-government philosophy and that it is spreading throughout the college and middle school communities.

"That is the most ridiculous thing I have ever heard," Jack said. "I know that, Jack. You know that. Angela knows that, but the cultural ministry is taking a hard look at these cross-cultural classes. And, they single you out, Jack, as a major source of this subversive threat."

"Source, hell, what did I do except teach a little English?"

"Oh, yeah, what about those dances in the moonlight along the Xiang, holding hands while walking back to the college, and buying those ice cream treats along the way? The China nights have a thousand eyes, Jack, you corrupter of innocent girls!"

"That is just plain silly," Jack replied. "All the teachers danced and walked together along the same street back to the school, and I bought all of them treats."

"That may be, Jack," Wolfman said, "but all of the students knew you and Angela got along quite well. Some are saying you were lovers."

"That is flagrant presumption." Jack said.

"No doubt," Wolfman agreed, "but it is what the police and ministry of culture believe that is important. And, Jack, this is

China, not your precious US of A; and Angela stands accused and is considered guilty!"

"No way, no way in hell, is she guilty of anything except being a nice Chinese woman who could charm the pants off anybody should she choose to do so. And, she did not choose to do so," Jack replied indignantly.

"Okay, Jack, if you say so," said Wolfman, "but the fact remains she is on trial and the next week does not look very pretty." "Wow, what can we do, Wolfman?" Jack asked.

"What is this 'we' stuff, Jack? She is your sweetie, not mine. I have put my neck on the block to contact you; however, you know how I hate these Gestapo types, just hate them! And, keep in mind, Jack, if you were here, you would be on trial with her as a co-conspirator! But, something very strange is going on here. There is a mystery about this trial that has not surfaced; nobody cares about the issues; these are non-issues. We need to keep our contact to a bare minimum, and if you were here, I could not be seen with you. You and Angela are my friends; I will help but we would have to meet secretly if you were here, and they would string me up in a New York minute if they knew. Keep our chat time for contact! Over and out!"

What started out for Jack as a routine day had turned into a nightmare as he thought about his last contact with Angela. She seemed stressed about her job. She was worried that the senior teachers and headmaster might fire her if she did not do well on her public teaching presentation before the faculty. Further, she expressed a desire to get out of the school that she said had some major problems.

Angela and Jack did get along; he often told her that she was the most beautiful woman in all of China. He asked her one time if she was actually Chinese for her facial features did not seem typically Chinese, but, yes, she was Han, number 56.

All the American male teachers were infatuated with her but she was aloof except for Jack. For some reason she lowered her defenses around him as she danced with him most of the time while the others watched. Other students danced with Jack but he always gravitated back to Angela; one time she said, "We are good together." Before too long it was clear they had a mutual attraction.

Jack was smitten. She was beautiful; she had long black hair; her face was attractive with piercing black eyes and a pretty smile. He asked about her ears one time. She replied, "They are cute, not too big, not too small." Later he asked about her breasts; she said, "They are very pretty, not too big, not too small, perfect for you." Jack did not have a chance.

He continued to think about their conversations long after he had left China. He asked her why she had not been more open to him when he was in China. Her reply was typical, "Oh, what do you expect, you silly man, a woman wants to be wooed and, big boy, in China the woman picks the man. You should have known before you left that I had picked you! It is not my fault you had to catch up to me. This is new China, not China of old. The new woman is independent but can be traditional if she wants. And, what of my reputation? I have to live here; you just fly away."

Jack knew thinking about past events would not change the present. Angela was in jail and charged with concocted allegations of subversive behavior and anti-government attitudes. Even though these charges did not ring true they were serious and carried potentially equally serious punishments. Only Angela and her accusers knew the real reason behind these damaging accusations. Jack had yet to develop a plan but he told Wolfman he would be in touch.

THE FAKE PASSPORT

"Kick this big bird in its tail," an impatient and confused Jack Thomas thought as the big plane began lumbering down the runway. He laid his head back and felt the vibrations increase until the doors of the overhead compartments were rattling. The roar of the powerful engines was almost deafening as the big plane built up thrust to take several hundred people, thousands of pounds of jet fuel, and a warehouse of luggage stored it its bowels into the air. It continued down the runway; Jack wondered how long it would be before it lifted into the air to start the 14 ½ hour trip to Shanghai. Finally, the plane cleared ground and Jack looked at the Chicago skyline for what might be his last look in a very long time. He was off to what he did not know.

The last message from Angela was an impassioned wish to get out of her school and to visit him in his beautiful state of Illinois. And, then, there were no more messages. Jack knew something had happened for he had worried about some comments in her last communication about how hard the job would be and that she was under enormous pressure to succeed. And, if she did not do well, they might fire her. But, he knew something greater than that had happened because the loss of a job could be discussed. Jack had approached the team leader, Micah Nussbaum, about going back into China. Mike had a passport with an extended visa, but Jack's had expired. He told Mike of Angela's desire to visit the United States.

"Well," that would leave one billion, 299, 999, 999 Chinese in China that also might want to visit the United States," he responded with his typical sarcasm.

"But, this is Angela we are talking about, not the 1.3 billion Chinese," Jack retorted, "and, I know something has happened to her!"

"So what! What the hell can we do about it? You know that what happens in China stays in China. How many times have I told you that?"

"Look, Jack, let me draw you a picture. Here is China. Here is the United States. What do you see in between? That is 9,000 miles plus of ocean. What do you propose to do about that? And, also what about those men in green uniforms that they call customs agents! What do you propose to do about them? Hell, Jack, they have laws about this sort of thing! Do you not know that? You cannot go into China and start tilting at windmills!"

"Damn it, Mike," Jack said, "I am not in the mood for your intellectualizing. I know there is an ocean there and that there are customs agents at each end. And, I know Jack Thomas cannot go into China anytime he wants, but Micah Nussbaum can."

With a quizzical look on his face and with his mouth hanging open, Mike asked, "What do you mean by that?"

"Look at us, Mike. We do not look that different. With a little cosmetics here and there, we could pass a visual check for passports," Jack explained.

"Oh, my god, you have lost it! You have really flipped out if you are thinking what I think you are thinking. Are you nuts? Please tell me today is your day to be temporarily insane!" Mike countered.

"Mike, think about it. I could use your passport, zip into China, find out what has happened, and come back in less than a week! How many times have you made a quick trip to China?"

"No, no, no! Absolutely not. You are exceeding any semblance of a rational mind. Think about what could happen to you if they caught you, not to mention that the educational program would be flushed. It has taken years to create this program for it had to overcome the suspiciousness and distrust they have of foreigners—and if someone did something like this? Jesus, Jack!"

"That is a good point! What would Jesus do for a friend in trouble? You do not pay any attention to Jesus anyway since you pretend to be a Jew!"

"Knock it off, Jack, "you know what I mean. If they caught you, you capitalist running dog, they would take you out and shoot you and before that they would cut off your balls, drill holes in your teeth, and then stuff your balls in your mouth!"

"Ah, Mike, you know better than that. If I am caught, I will be honest, plead my case of helping a friend, and throw myself upon their cultural sense of hospitality! I am not a threat; I want to find out what has happened to Angela!"

"Jack, you are one naïve, crazy son-of-a-bitch! Do you think for a moment they will give a rats ass about you and precious Angela? You silly bastard, anybody that lets somebody trick them into eating snake by calling it a "special fish" is one side of being plain dumb!"

"Well, that may be but you know Angela."

"Yes, we all know Angela, Jack, and yes, I know how she hypnotized all of us and, no, I do not want to be reminded again how she selected you, the great undeserving twit you are!"

"What if something has happened to her?"

"Do not go there, Jack, dammit, do not go there?"

"But, I have to, Mike, what if Angela has been fired or is in some other kind of trouble. Think of her in trouble in China, think of her in jail! She might have to . . ."

"Would you like something to drink? A flight attendant interrupted Jack's recollection of his conversation with his old friend."

"Yes, orange juice, please."

"Would you like that with ice?"

"Yes, thank you!"

His meditation was broken but he returned briefly to think how he had gotten Nussbaum's passport and as he left the office, Mike said with a sickly smile, "Good luck, Jack," and gave him a thumb's up gesture. For all his bull and big mouth, Jack knew Mike's heart was in the right place.

Jack summed up the situation. He had spent one month in China, taught English improvement classes to Chinese English teachers, and had made several dear friends. He remembered when he first met Angela; she was in the front of the classroom of his first class, and after he had written several things on the blackboard, she said something like, "Hey, Jack, it would be better if you would print!" He laughed to himself as he remembered looking at her smiling face and saying, "Yes, of course, I will print!" Now, he was entering, hopefully, China with someone else's passport, to go to the same place he was in the summer, to find out what had happened, and he had no idea of what he would do.

He remembered more things about Angela. At the end of the day, she would take charge of the classroom, have the students to clean the room, put materials in order, and prepare the classroom for the next school day. She told him she was his guide in Changsha and she led him through the old, narrow, rambling streets of Changsha that went out of this traditional part of town. This was a group effort as the other teachers went along as well. All of them went to the Xiang River and to the park where they danced. He remembered dancing to traditional Chinese songs, and how she would tell him the story of the song; he could see her long black hair flying in the breeze as they moved around the concrete pillars in the middle of the dance area. And, they walked up and down the riverfront, "I am sorry, Jack, for the bad smell," she said at the lower end of the river away from the park.

One afternoon Angela came to Jack and asked, "Are you going to the river tonight?"

"Yes, we probably will."

"Well, these friends have asked me over to their place. I do not want to go, but I do not know . . ."

"How to say, No!" "Yeah, I do not know how to say 'no'."

Jack recounted how he fought against showing disappointment but laughed and said, "That is all right, do not worry about it; we will go another night."

Angela smiled and said, "Okay!"

That night, when the crowd gathered to go to the river, she was there and as the group moved down the narrow street, Jack and Angela managed to find themselves side-by-side as they always had.

One night they had walked ahead of the group, "It does not matter," Angela said. As they waited for the others to catch up, Bradley rode down the street on a bicycle with a student riding on the back. Everybody laughed when they looked at the bicycle and Bradley said, "Hell, you can buy a new bicycle at the shop across the street for $20. And, it is a good one too. Why not buy one; you can use it here and give it to someone when you leave."

"Let's go." And, with that Jack and Angela and the others went to the bicycle shop to pick out bicycles. Jack asked Angela to pick out one for he had already decided to give it to her when he left; this way she would pick out one she favored. Bradley started something; soon five members of the team had bought bicycles. Angela was a superb dancer and she taught Jack how to spin around with their arms over their heads. She would say with a melodic kind of purring in her voice, "I am so happy." One night she commented, "We are good together." That night ended as the other nights with the group walking back to the college down the little street. Jack talked to Bradley that night about how he and Angela had never been alone and that there always were other people around. Bradley said, "Well, do you know that Angela and Rose have never been kissed?"

"You are kidding!"

"No, that is what they told the girls," Bradley said. ("The girls" was the code name for the females on the team.) The girls gathered a lot of information from the Chinese teachers because the Chinese wanted to know about dating, marriage, and a whole lot of other things that fall under the heading of girl talk.

Jack told Bradley he was going to do something about the fact that Angela had never been kissed. Bradley asked, "What are you going to do?"

"Kiss her."

The next night when all of the usual bunch got back from the river, Jack asked Angela to visit his room on the first floor of the dormitory. She hesitated but he said, "It is all right; I am inviting you and you are my guest."

As they entered the room Angela walked to the middle of the room near a little round table with two chairs near the wall with two beds and headboards on the opposite wall of the room. She stood there and looked around the room.

"Why not sit down," Jack asked. He felt a little peculiar about asking her to sit when there were two beds in the room.

She turned and faced him and said, "No, I cannot stay very long."

Jack walked up close to her and gently gathered her face between both his hands, looked directly into her eyes, and slowly lowered his mouth to hers and firmly kissed her. After a brief moment, he looked again into her eyes and she did not show any emotion or any reaction that he could notice.

"I have to be going," she said.

"Are you worried that someone may have seen you come into the room? (He thought of the little dorm mother.)

"Yes."

He hurriedly opened the door and accompanied her to the stairs that led to the upper rooms in the dorm. And as she went up the stairs he told her, "Good night."

He wanted the dorm mother to see him and to see that Angela was on her way to her dorm floor. As he went to bed Jack worried that he may have violated some norm with Angela. Mike said the Chinese have little privacy. What would be said about her going into his room if only less than a minute? He tossed in his sleep that night. He wondered if anyone would try to do anything about it but finally decided to hell with it; they better not even try.

THE TRIAL

"Let's go, pigface!" Chief Investigator Liao yelled to his subordinate, Assistant Investigator Chan. Then he put the phone down, got up from his chair, and told Chan they had an investigation in Changsha County about a charge of subversive activities. Chan smiled and was delighted for these forays into the country to investigate violations of the Cultural Ministry were always exciting and got him away from his desk. Also, he dearly loved his seemingly irascible boss who used various pet names for him.

Liao rescued Chan from a boring future with the honor guard around the Forbidden City in Beijing. Chan was a handsome man who always had a smile on his face and that was his undoing while he was an honor guard. He could not maintain his sober face and when he saw ridiculous looking foreigners he laughed. When tourists saw this, he inevitably ended up in picture taking, especially if there were young ladies in the group for Chan attracted girls as bees to honey. The commandant of the guards warned him about this but Chan could not help himself.

One day, when the commandant was disciplining Chan, Liao was within listening distance and he moved closer to see what was happening. What he saw was a crusty old man chewing out a handsome young man who reflected the new China Liao was so much wanting to help create. After the unpleasant session was over Liao approached the commandant and asked what was wrong. The commandant immediately recognized Liao for Liao was a well-placed party member and worked in the Division of Criminal Enforcement of the Ministry of Culture.

"Ah, these young people just have no respect," the old officer said. Liao could tell he was scarred from many campaigns and was put out to pasture in this easy job. Liao asked him if he could help him and the old officer straightened with pride and responded that he would help his country in any possible way. Liao told him he needed a young assistant, a presentable looking person with a personality that could get along with a variety of people such as the different groups of foreigners who tour the Forbidden City. The grizzled old officer thought for a moment and then his eyes sparkled, and he said, "I have just the right person for you!"

"Good! When can I meet him and see if he will be interested in taking another assignment?"

"How about on the next hour, and leave it to me; he will be interested."

Liao thanked him respectfully and turned away to kill time until the next hour. Chief Investigator Liao was a product of the new China. He was educated in Marxism, Leninism, the new economics, and most importantly, he had worked in the government close to Deng Xiaoping. The new China was a passion to him. His parents and grandparents suffered through the old regimes, and he did not believe that was the best choice for the future. He wanted to see people live well, free from fear of government officials, and to be better educated. And Liao believed China should open its borders, open its mind and eyes to the rest of the world. To be selective, to be sure, but he always remembered what Deng Xiaoping said. "It does not matter what color the cat is if it catches the mouse."

On the hour Liao approached the commandant's headquarters to see the old officer with a young man in tow with his duffle. The old officer smiled broadly, exposing worn teeth and proudly announced, "Here he is, sir!" Liao looked briefly at the young soldier who had snapped to attention and had saluted and gave him a casual wave of his hand and told the old commandant, "I believe he will do." He hid any trace of excitement in his voice. Thus began what was to become a wonderful working relationship between Chief Investigator Liao and soon-to-become Assistant Investigator Chan.

As Liao led Chan toward the official vehicle waiting for them, he asked him, "Do you know who I am?"

"Only by reputation, sir," Chan replied with his ever-present smile. Liao thought to himself that we may have to work on that smile of his.

The subversive case involved a school teacher in the Changsha County Middle School that the headmaster had charged with committing subversive activities and having anti-government attitudes. Her crime was that of being overly friendly with American teachers in a summer professional development program to improve her level of English. The charge further listed too close fraternization of a personal nature with one of the teachers. In brief, the charges against the middle school teacher were that she was corrupting the Chinese youth with American economic and political ideas. And as she was responsible for political training of the students, she was in a sensitive area of education. The case intrigued Liao for he, of course, was familiar with western economic ideas and particularly with what he called American bloated capitalism that allowed chief executive officers of the industry to engage in a feeding frenzy upon the productivity of workers. He knew of excessive profits, insider training, and the Enrons of American industry. Further, he knew how peoples' retirement funds had been so depleted in the last few years. It angered him that the government allowed these things to happen. He thought that if only that had happened in China, what could he do? But them he began to despair as he thought about how they had so much over there and how they acted like hogs at the trough, and in China, there were so many . . . "Sir, sir." He was jarred out of his revelry when Chan asked him whether or not this case was going to involve a typical trial setting.

After a moment's reflection, Liao said, "Yes. I want to see and hear what is going on. We approved these cross-cultural programs; now, we need to see what kind of fruit that heave brought us. And, Chan, you are going to sit as first chair, the headmaster is going to be second chair, and a college official is going to be third chair. See to it!"

Chan knew how serious Liao was from their experience of working together. He knew he was in a pensive thoughtful mood for he did not call him one of his pet names, and he was in a no-nonsense mode of giving directions. Chan knew to let him think things through when he was in one of these moods, not out of fear but out of respect, for he too began to become more thoughtful about what was ahead.

They were the perfect working team. Liao was always in the background, observing, planning, directing, and Chan was the frontman, the one who took charge and barked orders with authority. Chan had also developed his serious, do-not-fool-with-me-face too. It was a good strategy. Chan could act without having to consider all the things going on around him, and Liao could reflect upon "the big picture" and not have to act. They were connected with mobile phones; both had discussed their roles and understood them.

When they arrived at the local Ministry of Culture building, Chan immediately got to work and got the trial room set up, and the adjacent soundproof room checked out for Liao's place of observance. There was no way anyone in the trail room could know Liao was observing the proceedings. Liao would wander around the building and often talk with custodians or secretaries and then show up in the observation room unseen about fifteen minutes before the trial would start. He particularly did not want the headmaster to see him because he had known him for about ten years. He also knew Chan had both of other chairs in a preparatory room to go over issues of the case before the trial.

The trial started at ten o'clock on Tuesday morning. The three chairs took their positions seconds before ten o'clock, and exactly at the hour a cultural ministry official escorted the accused into the chair confronting the trial officers; the chair for the accused was on a little elevated platform with wooden fence and gate around it.

When the judge appeared, everyone briefly stood and then took their seats. The judge took charge and asked that the charges be read. Liao observed from his viewing room.

Chan took advantage of the time it took to read the charges to study the person in the chair confronting them. What he saw was a respectful young lady with a hurt bewildered look on her face with swollen eyes. She sat erect, her mouth was closed, and she had a dignified countenance. Her face looked as though it should be smiling; her head was surrounded with long black hair. She appeared to be from a small city or village rather than from a large urban center. Chan began to soften, but he knew he could not as he thought, "Let's see what sins she has committed!"

After the charges were read, Chan led the questioning and asked, "Is your name Angela? And is this your English name?"

"Yes, sir," she replied.

"You do not need to call me sir as this is a people's court," Chan replied. "Your respect is noted," he added. He wondered what Liao would think of that.

"Angela," Chan began, "We are here to find out the truth of these charges and to understand why they have been brought against you! We will investigate and will determine if the evidence produced finds them true or false. Do you trust the people's court to be fair with you?" Chan looked directly into her eyes when he asked this question, but immediately, he wished he had not, for when her eyes met his, they had a trapped pleading look.

"Yes," was the quiet compliant reply.

"Thank you," Chan said spontaneously. Damn! Why did I say that? And his eyes brushed past the hidden window Liao used from his vantage observation position.

The first series of questions established the facts that Angela taught political theories as well as English and had had the experience of summer professional development classes in the Changsha Education College with American teachers. Her voice gained strength as Chan guided her through these basic information questions as politely and considerately as he could. Angela visibly gained confidence as her trust in him increased. However, Chan knew there were tough questions ahead as he had done this so many times before; gain their trust only to knock their legs out from under them later. He dreaded the next questions he knew he must ask.

"Did the American professors teach subjects such as US history and political systems?"

For the first time, a smile appeared on the accused's face. "Yes."

"Did these professors talk to you privately about their political, economic, and historical interpretations?"

"Some of them did; most of them did not."

"Of those who did, do you remember them specifically and what they said?"

"Yes."

"Which ones do you remember?"

"The history teacher."

"And what do you remember about what he said?"

"He spoke about what he called the consumerism of the new China. He was amazed that he saw kids with toys and how people ate popsicles and ice cream bars. The happiness of the people impressed him, and he talked about how they smiled and waved and yelled "hello"! He also mentioned his observations about how hard Chinese people worked, and he told one story several times about how he saw a little girl help her father push a coal cart across the Changsha Bridge."

Chan glanced furtively at the special window and at the clock, just as the judge called for lunch recess and for the trial to resume at one o'clock. This lunch break allowed Chan and Liao to adjust their approaches to the trial. Liao suggested Chan continue to see the depths of political theory these teachers brought into this cross-cultural program.

The trial resumed promptly at one o'clock. Chan stood, looked at Angela, and asked, "Did this professor have any explanation about the new consumerism he observed?"

"Yes."

"Could you tell us about it?"

"Sorry," Angela almost laughed. "Yes, he suggested it was a consequence of Deng Xiaoping and his modernizations in China. Deng opened China to the world and trade; the world responded amazingly, and as a result, people's livelihood and standard of living improved. He mentioned how many people had electric washing machines, private telephones and home computers, air conditioning, and refrigerators. And he said this was based upon Sun Yat-Sen's idea of "livelihood" that the people should live better lives."

Chan appered to be grasping for questions when he asked with a puzzled look on his face, "Did this professor say anything else about Sun Yat-Sen?"

"He talked about how Sun had ended the period of emperors' rule and encouraged nationalism in China, and how he wanted the people to have more democracy, and how he wanted the people to live better lives or have greater livelihood. He compared Sun to Abraham Lincoln of America."

Unable to restrain himself any longer, Chan asked, "Why did he compare him to Abraham Lincoln?"

"Because," Angela began, "Lincoln talked of one nation and one people during the American Civil War, and he talked also of government by, of, and for the people. Sun had similar ideas with his views on nationalism, democracy, and livelihood. And there followed an extended civil war in China with Chiang Kai Shek who followed Sun and Chairman Mao who led the communists. And Lincoln was a nationalist also—an American nationalist."

Damn, she has turned into a parrot, thought Chan, and said, "What did this professor have to say about Chiang Kai Shek and Chairman Mao?"

"He described Chiang as a throwback almost to the days of the emperors with bloated capitalism and government bureaucratic corruption; he said Madame Chiang was even worse. He said that American support of Chiang was one of the greatest mistakes in foreign policy in its history.

The headmaster objected, "Must we continue to listen to this history recitation?"

The judge overruled his objection and said, "The question was asked, and she should be allowed to answer it. Would you continue with this man's views of Chairman Mao?"

"It is his opinion that Chairman Mao will be remembered as one of the greatest leaders of the Chinese people who genuinely had the peoples' interests at heart. He quoted the chairman's speech about how the Chinese people have stood up; he believes Chairman Mao and his management skills had been necessary or the new China would not be possible. He laughed about "The Little Red Book" and called it Management 101; he also said the chairman could have been one of the richest men in the world but died with only a modest estate and asked that there not by any memorial built to his memory. He also spoke of the two great burdens of Chinese people—imperialism and feudalism and how the chairman freed the people of both."

At the end of this testimony, Liao rose to his feet, grabbed the mobile phone, and called Chan and told him, "Find out who this Mao-quoting professor is!"

Chan asked of the accused, "You say this is an American professor, yet he seems to be a Chinese historian. What is his name?"

Angela glowed as she answered that his name was Jack Thomas and that he had studied Chinese History as well as United States History.

The judge noted the time and adjourned the trial until nine o'clock the next morning.

After the official escorted Angel back to the holding cell, Liao contacted Chan. "There is something going on here. I sense that all is not what it appears to be in the trial and with the accusations. Bring the headmaster and college official to the viewing room!"

Chan complied immediately. When the headmaster saw Liao, he greeted him with, "Hello, my old friend!"

Liao responded with an emotional level Chan seldom saw, "Do not 'old friend' me, you piece of dog turd! What kind of crap are you trying to pull off? What are you doing?"

Not taken aback at all, the headmaster said, "This woman is a subversive influence on the students and fraternized with foreigners."

Liao again responded with fury, "You are exactly what is wrong with China, your old technique of getting rid of someone just because you may not like them has no place in today's China What did this person do except participate in a cultural exchange program that I helped start and approved, I might add? She is a produce of that program, and it appears to be a good product!"

"Yes, but you have not heard all the testimony. There are examples of criticisms of Chairman Mao."

"So what! Was not Mao voted to have been only seventy percent correct in his actions? That leaves thirty percent of his policies open to criticism, dogface!"

"But I am the headmaster, and I say she is subversive. She is under my authority—the authority the party gave me to run this school."

A powerful part member, Liao, exploded. "Do not hide behind the part. The party does not want old pieces of crap like you cluttering the progress of modern China. There is no place for this old vengeful behavior. Do not forget who you are talking, dog piss, because I could have your head for fraudulent charges and incompetent management."

The headmaster grew more respectful as he offered the college official as testimony to more wrongdoing. And suddenly, he discovered how he could refer to Liao as sir.

Liao did not want to challenge local party officials, but he knew there was something rotten about this case, and he finally said, "Let's continue the trial, hear the rest of the testimony and set a time to make a final resolution."

The next morning at nine o'clock, the trial resumed. All parties positioned themselves as before. Chan opened the questioning and asked Angela if the professors had criticized Chinese leaders.

"Yes," she replied. They expressed the view that Chairman Mao reached a point when he was a detriment to the revolution. They argued that Mao was responsible for Chinese nationalism and independence, but then the party turned inwardly upon itself with the cultural revolution."

Liao was spellbound as he listed to her testimony. The headmaster again protested the history lesson. Again, the judge said, "You initiated these charges and investigation. We will exhaust all testimony."

Chan asked, "Was this criticism disrespectful to the memory of the chairman?"

"No, the professor mentioned the vote of seventy percent approval of Mao. He suggested there was a lack of procedure for the transfer of power."

"So he said good things and bad things about the chairman?"

"Yes," Angela said. "He also referred to Deng Xiaoping who said that donkeys move slowly but they do move."

Chan asked, "How did he describe Deng?"

"He believed Deng Xiaoping was a logical succession to Mao. Mao had achieved Chinese nationalism; Deng was improving democracy and Chinese livelihood. The professor said that neither Marxism nor unregulated capitalism would fit China, and he believed Deng thought the same way as Deng is famous for his statement that it does not matter if the cat is black or white as long as it catches the mouse. Deng ushered in the new China as he opened China's doors and minds to the world."

"Do you feel American teachers taught anything subversive?"
"No."

The headmaster interrupted, "Of course, she would say that because of the inappropriate fraternization with them!" Chan asked him to ask questions.

The headmaster started. "How often did you meet with the teachers?"

"Every day, during the teaching session."

"Did you meet with them socially after school hours?"

"The college asked class leaders to escort them whenever they left the campus and to serve as guides to show them around Changsha. Also, the school provided some money to pay for certain entertainments such as dances at the river part."

"Did you spend time alone with any of the professors?"

"No."

The headmaster then asked, "How can you explain the report of the dormitory mother that you entered the living quarters of Jack Thomas and Bradley Crawford?"

Angela responded irritably that she did not consider less than a minute as spending time alone.

The headmaster pursued the question, "What was the purpose of the visit?"

To see how they lived, to see their western private bathroom and to see how different it was from the students' quarters."

"Are you sure that is why you went into their room?"

The judge commented, "This question has already been answered!"

The headmaster continued his line of questions, "Did you spend time with the teachers during non-teaching days?"

"Yes."

"What did you do?"

"A group of five of us bicycled to Orange Island to have a picnic and to take pictures."

The judge adjourned the trial until the afternoon at the same time as before.

Liao more than ever believed this was a fake trial with fake charges. After the first rounds of testimony and questions, what had emerged? A Mao-quoting American professor who had a close relationship with a beautiful Chinese woman. This was laughable. Was this the subversive conspiracy the headmaster alleged? This was a show trial!

Liao called Chan to have the headmaster and college official to again meet in the viewing room. When they gathered, Liao asked the group they believed the trial was progressing. The headmaster expressed disappointment at Chan's lenient line of questions. Chan was not getting at the conspiratorial aspects of her behavior but had opened the door for her to confuse the real issues of influence peddling of American economic and political ideologies. He suggested a stricter line of questioning. The college official apologized for not recognizing subversive tendencies among the teachers.

After listening intently to their comments, Liao took some time to sit quietly and to meditate. Chan knew what was coming next; the volcano would erupt, and it would not be pretty. Liao began to speak softly and slowly; he talked of his dreams of a new China, a China of better educated people, a China of higher living standards, and he specifically described his support for the English language program at Changsha Education College. He advocated bilingual curriculums where Chinese students would study histories of other countries in the language of that country. He mentioned the US history classes in Changsha High School taught in English with Chinese teachers. And he proudly mentioned the US History Advanced Placement program.

"Do you see what scholars they are? Do you see the advantages they have in the world? This is the heart and core of the new China. He commented how China had always had problems accepting ideas from the outside world. This teacher on trial is a product of this program; this student is one of China's finest, and she is accused of being subversive. His voice now began to rise with almost a rumble of an earthquake; Chan had seen it before. This student is being tried for learning what she was supposed to learn? This trial"—his voice reached a crescendo—"is bullshit! The trial could undermine this whole cultural exchange program. It is a sham trial that harks back to the old days we are leaving behind. And I, mister headmaster, you stream of monkey piss, am not accepting it!"

"You want a stricter approach; so do I. there is something here we do not know. Mister Headmaster, do you want to tell us what you are trying to accomplish here?"

The flustered headmaster said that he was standing behind his subversive and conspiratorial charges.

Liao looked at the headmaster and said softly, "That is what I thought you would say, and if you believe, you miserable bastard, that I am going to let you destroy this program, you are dumber than I had thought. Chan, take off your gloves! First, assure the accused she will be protected and treated respectfully, but she must tell us what has been going on at that school. Tell her she has to be a hundred percent truthful, and she will be treated fairly. Then start the hard questions; you know what to do!"

The trial resumed at the designated time. The official led Angela to her chair to face her accusers. For some reason, Chan stood up and briefly looked around the courtroom and casually walked and stood directly in front of Angela. He began, "You said earlier you had faith this trial would be fair. Do you still believe that?"

He looked directly into her eyes that reflected the look of a frightened, trapped animal as she said firmly, "Yes, I do."

Chan paused as he thought to himself if this gorgeous creature is guilty of this crap, my grandpa was a monkey. He then asked if she had been treated well; was she comfortable?

Again, she replied firmly, "Yes."

Chan turned slowly and resumed his seat at the table and asked Angela if she understood the importance of answering questions with one hundred percent truthfulness.

"Yes," she said.

"Is there anything in your previous testimony you wish to change or to add?"

Angela paused and thoughtfully said, "No, not really."

Chan let her answer linger a moment and said, "Not really? Does that mean there is something?"

"I did not consider it important."

"We will determine its importance," said a firm Chan in full control. "What is it you want to change or to add?"

She blushed as she recalled her testimony about visiting Jack Thomas in his dormitory room.

"Yes, yes," Chan encouraged her.

"Jack Thomas kissed me in his room," she said.

"He kissed you?" Chan repeated.

"Yes."

"Did you resist him?" Chan asked.

"No."

"Did he force himself upon you?"

"No."

"How did he kiss you?" Chan continued.

Angela was flushed as she said, "He walked up to me, held my face in his hands, and kissed me!"

"Did you try to get out of the room or to run away?"

"No, I stood still in the middle of the room."

Chan persisted, "Why did you not try to escape?"

Angela's face was now blood-red as she said, "Because I wanted it!"

Pandemonium broke out in the courtroom. Chan stood, looked at Angela, and smiled his famous smile; she smiled back at him.

The judge banged his gavel and insisted on order. Liao called Chan and asked, "Is this your version of stricter questions, and is this my tough Bulldog prosecutor? Do you want to go back to honor guard?"

Chan replied, "I am sorry, but I could not control myself," and he laughed.

At the other end, Liao told Chan to call for a recess and then Chan heard laughter on the line as Liao tried to tell him to bring the two donkeys to his private room. Chan had never heard Liao laugh so.

The judge called for a recess. Chan, the headmaster, and the college official assembled with Liao. Liao started and said what a mess Chan had made of the trial. Then he said, "When I told you to get tough, I meant for you to ask questions about the school, ask about what happened there. What caused this?"

The headmaster knew what they would find out and suddenly made an unusual request. "Sir, in view of the situation, I feel it is wise to drop the charges!"

Liao looked at him and finally spoke, "What are you afraid of? Are you afraid we might find out about your level of incompetence?"

"No, no, it seems everybody is in her favor and would not convict her of anything!"

Liao knew he was hiding something, but at this moment, he did not care. He said, "I will give you six months to make changes in your school. I believe you are capable to turn this situation around. This is the price you must pay for us to drop the charges!"

Liao allowed the headmaster to save face, and also to get the Cultural Ministry out of this mess. It was a winning situation for everyone.

When court reconvened, the judge said, "Young lady, I am charging you with contempt of court!"

Chan jumped to his feet and said, "I object!"

"Objection noted, sit down!"

"I still object!"

Chan's phone caught his eye. "Sit down, stupid, and shut up!" Chan obeyed.

"Young lady," the judge droned on. "I am charging you with contempt of court! You must join me in my chambers and stand very still and quiet in the middle of the room! This trial is adjourned until Monday at nine o'clock in the morning."

All hell broke loose again as the judge walked to his chambers with Angela in tow. When they got into the room, the judge removed his robe and walked toward Angela, and took her hands in his and said, "Do not worry. I will not kiss you. I have known your father for years; he is my friend and a good party member. Please tell him hello for me. I am so sorry for this mess has happened."

He then told Angela she was to be released to go to her family for the weekend and that she should appear in court on Monday morning at nine o'clock.

THE PLAN

Most of the people in the courtroom were the customary loafers and thrill seekers that hang out to watch trials except for one person who did not fit into this crowd. Wolfman followed every stage of the trial because of his friendship with Angela and Jack. He told Jack the trial would probably last until after the weekend.

Jack's plane arrived in Changsha late Friday night. He told Wolfman to meet him near the dancing area on the Xiang. Jack would be there after the dancing had cleared out; he would sit on one of the park benches and look at the river. Wolfman could approach him when there was a minimum of people around. By 11:30pm, Jack had taken up his position and appeared to be resting as though he had been on a long walk. About fifteen minutes later, Wolfman sauntered along and took a seat about twenty feet from Jack.

"Hiya," Wolfman said.

"Hi, yourself," Jack responded. "What has been going on?"

Wolfman quickly brought Jack up to speed. He ended his briefing with the story about the contempt of court charge. He then told Jack he had seen Angela leave the courtroom with one of her family members. That was all he knew.

Jack asked if he knew where Angela's family lived and if he could contact her.

"Sure. I know exactly where she is with this family member."

"Good. Here is the plan. I need to smuggle Angela out of China!"

"Oh, really," Wolfman said. "Just like that; you are taking Angela out of country! Are you crazy?"

"Well, I know somebody somewhere smuggles things into the country so why not smuggle something out of the country? Most of their legal system is geared to catch something coming in, not going out," Jack replied.

Wolfman was quiet and pensive. He had never thought of it exactly that way.

Jack continued, "What I need is the 'king of smugglers' who would help smuggle two people out. It is not contraband we are talking about. I am here legally after coming out through customs; however, that might change and if it were to change what would be wrong about trying to get out if country because they would kick me out anyway? Of course, if I am helping a fugitive from justice and a citizen to escape, that would up the ante."

"My idea, Wolfman, is to travel the river system until we can reach a port. Then we can transfer to some freighter whose captain would like some extra money and is not too concerned about how he gets it. Again, smuggle out, not smuggle in. Who cares about a freighter leaving the country? The concern is about the ones coming into the country," Jack elaborated.

Wolfman again looked puzzled, especially when Jack said, "I know you have some questionable underworld contacts. What is needed is a fast, run-down-looking boat like the ones tied up on this river, but one that is already used in some smuggling activities. Money is the incentive."

"There is such a captain, I am told," said Wolfman, "who might be interested. I can make a contact. How much money are we talking about?"

"Let's start at three thousand dollars. That can go higher. And there is one other thing. You must contact Angela, tell her to pack a light bag for traveling with some food. And get her here this morning. Time is very important!"

Wolfman made a call, talked briefly, and reported, "There is such a captain right here along the riverbank. His boat is in the first slip from the pier; he has a mean reputation, but he is willing to talk to you. He goes by the name of Hogjowl; you will know when you see him. There will be two lights turned on; go down and see him. He is expecting you."

Wolfman then took off to pick up Angela.

Jack went to the boat and walked very carefully across a gangplank that was between the pier and the boat. When the door of the boat opened, Hogjowl presented an awful picture, his jaws and jowls hanged down, he was unshaven, and there was a smell of cheap booze. Perfect, thought Jack. Hogjowl spoke a little English, "What you want, American?"

"I need transportation for two people."

"Why not take bus, train, or plane?"

"Romance," said Jack. "We want a romantic river cruise."

"On an old boat like mine?" Hogjowl asked suspiciously.

"Your boat has a reputation of being a good one and fast, even though it looks like the others. Why is your boat so fast?" Jack asked.

Hogjowl smiled and said, "My business!"

"So," Jack said, "you are in business, and this is a business proposition. I will pay you four thousand dollars to take us to Shanghai."

"Hah! Fuel costs money. I must have eight thousand dollars."

After haggling, the fee was six thousand dollars. Jack was pleased with his bargaining.

Now, they waited for Angela.

About two thirty in the morning, Wolfman's car slowly came into view and stopped in a dark place along the street. Jack watched from behind a tree.

Slowly, Angela and then Wolfman got out of the car. There was a little traffic, and they saw no police cars. When Jack thought it was safe, he stopped from behind the tree and said, "Hi, Angela."

Angela responded with, "Hello, Jack, what a way to meet! Should we do this more often? What are you doing here anyway?"

"I am here to smuggle you out of the country."

"What! I am supposed to go with you out of the country just as my trial is almost over? Why?"

Jack replied, "You have powerful enemies here. These enemies will not let you resume your teaching career. They will get at you in some other way. Your life will be miserable if you stay, and it could be dangerous for you. And you may get some jail time."

"Oh," Angela replied. "Are you not exaggerating? And, by the way, glad to see you."

"No, I do not think so. And neither does Wolfman. And glad to see you too."

"But I am to show up at court Monday morning to hear my sentence!"

"Yes, and they may give you some time in jail and add some other things to your so-called crimes."

"What would they give me if they caught me leaving the country?" Angela asked.

"Hopefully that will not happen," Jack said.

"Angela," Wolfman said, "we have a good plan to smuggle you out of the country with less risk than what you face if you stay. You know how I distrust these people. You have better chances with Jack, believe me."

"Should I trust you that much, Jack?" Angela asked.

"I have put myself at great risk to come here. Does that not warrant trust?" Jack said.

Angela was quiet for a moment and then quickly made up her mind. "Let's go," she said. "Almost anything would be better than that hellhole where I was teaching. And whatever comes our way, we will confront together."

Wolfman and Jack embraced. Jack said, "I can never replay you."

"No problem. Get out of country—for me, for Angela, and for you. Good luck!"

Angela kissed Wolfman on the cheek and said, "Do not get any ideas, Wolfie; I am with Jack."

Wolfman laughed heartily and said, "It has always been so; we all knew." And then, he asid something out of character. "May God go with you?"

Angela and Jack made their way to the boat and waved at Wolfman who watched them enter the boat.

Hogjowl fired up his powerful engine, dropped the mooring lines, and slowly eased the boat out of the slip into the murky depths of the Xiang. He was an experienced "river rat" and smoothly navigated the boat downstream. His wife prepared a place for Jack and Angela to rest and to get some much-needed sleep. With the quiet humming of the diesel, they were soon sleeping. Hogjowl asked for coffee as it was going to be a long night. When they cleared the city, his wife spared him at the wheel.

The sunrise found them making good progress. They did not move near the top speed of the boat as that would attract attention. They were several miles from Changsha on the first leg of their journey to Shanghai.

THE OTHER PASSPORT

Chief Investigator Liao had looked forward to a peaceful weekend in Changsha. But, on Saturday, customs at Shanghai Airport contacted him about a suspicious passport. His first reaction was to ask, "Why are you contacting me?" The customs agent said that the person was going to Changsha and that another person with the same name was already in Changsha. That got Liao's attention, and he asked how that would be possible. The agent added more to the story and told Liao the person in question was the leader of American teachers who taught at Changsha Education College. At this bit of news, Liao stood up and told the customs agent to stand by.

He thought for a few moments and contacted Chan to have the helicopter ready to go as soon as possible. He then told the customs agent to expect him as soon as a flight time permitted.

When they arrived at the airport, customs agents brought Liao and Chan up-to-date on the situation. They detained Michael Nussbaum; they said that he had a story about his passport and had not deviated from it. They ushered Liao and Chan into the room where they were holding Mike. Liao walked up close to him, looked at him for a moment as to size him up, and extend his hand and introduced himself.

Liao then said, "I understand you have a passport problem."

"Yes, sir, I do," Mike responded respectfully.

"Perhaps we can resolve this problem. You say your passport was stolen or lost?"

"Yes, I do not know whether it was lost or stolen."

"And, you want us to believe you do not know."

Mike firmly said, "Yes, I do not know."

"Do you know that as Chief Investigator of Cultural Affairs I am responsible for the program you have at Changsha Education College?"

"I have heard your name before," said Mike.

"You know then that with a stroke of a pen I could end that program?"

Mike responded, "Yes, I suppose so."

"And, you do not want to change your story?"

"No, I do not want to change my story."

"Very well," Liao said, "Are you comfortable, are you hungry, thirsty, or have any needs?" He said to the customs agent, "Will you see to Mr. Nussbaum's needs? Whatever he needs, make sure he gets it; make him comfortable! I will return in 30 minutes," Liao said on his way out of the office.

When he was outside the office, he looked back at Mike, laughed, and said to the customs agent, "He is lying through his teeth. Look at him sweat."

The customs agent told him they had gotten information about Mike from U. S. authorities. He was a former police officer who had worked on vice in a large U. S. city and was a tough customer; he knew all the tricks of interrogation and how to deal with criminals. Liao said that it was not a matter of forcing him to talk because there was a great leverage over him, the continued success of the educational program in Changsha.

"We will try a different approach," said Liao.

After thirty minutes, Liao and the customs agent went back into the room and Liao looked at Mike thoughtfully before he said anything and then asked, "May I call you Mike?"

"Yes, please do."

"Mike, I apologize for this inconvenience and interrogation when we all know something unusual happened to your passport. I ask you as one investigator to another do you trust me if I were to give you my word on something?"

"Yes, I believe I can trust you," said Mike.

"Here is the situation, Mike. You are in a position to help us. You have committed no crime; we have no legal reason to hold you except that we think you can help us. Are you protecting someone? Do you think you are protecting the educational program at Changsha? This is my word of trust, Mike. You are free to go but I may cancel the program at Changsha if you do not help us. No matter what you tell us, you are free to go and we will escort you and help you make up for your lost time. We will be grateful to you if you help us; we are on the same side, Mike. That is my word of trust. Are you ready for the question? I will give you a few minutes to think about it. Your answer, I believe, will help us a great deal," Liao concluded.

Liao then asked Mike the question, "What happened to your passport?" When Liao looked at Mike, he knew he had used the right approach.

Mike said, "Okay. I will tell you the whole story and the program will be saved?"

"Yes. My word," Liao replied.

Mike then told the whole story and Liao was visibly affected because he immediately connected it to the trial at Changsha. "Mike, do you know Angela?"

"Yes, very well. She was an outstanding student in the program."

"Did you know she is on trial for subversive activities and anti-government attitudes?"

Mike answered with a shocked expression, "No, I did not. I only heard that something had possibly happened to her."

Liao continued to question him, "Do you think she is capable of subversive activities and corruption of her students?"

"Hell, no," Mike exploded. "Maybe when pigs can fly. Nothing could be more ridiculous about Angela. She was a star graduate of Changsha Education College.

"Those are my feelings as well," said Liao. "Would Jack Thomas be capable of subversive influence over his students such as Angela?"

Mike laughed and said that Jack and Angela had other interests and had no time for subversive activities.

Liao smiled at this answer and said, "Thank you, Mike, I am pleased you chose to help us. And, for the record, regardless of your answer, I would not have closed the Changsha program. It is part of the new China."

"Now, Mike, this is over. I have a helicopter. Would you honor us to fly with us to Changsha?

Mike said, "Yes. It will be my pleasure, Chief Investigator."

They stood, shook hands, and laughed.

MONDAY MORNING COURTROOM

Monday morning in the courtroom started as it usually did on any other morning. Secretaries, recorders, and the usual staff were getting ready for the morning session. Liao and Chan arrived at the fashionable time; the school headmaster and college president are not far behind. The judge has entered his chambers and prepared to emerge to preside over the proceedings. At the stroke of 9:00am the judge strolls out, everyone in the court rises, the judge takes his seat and motions for everyone to be seated. The judge asks for the first case which is the case of subversive activities, anti-government attitudes, and contempt of court charges against Angela. However, there is a problem as she is not present.

The judge asks if she has contacted anyone to say she would not be there. She has not contacted anyone. After a few minutes the judge ruled her absent without authorization and returned to his chambers with Chan, the headmaster, and college president. Liao also joined the group.

Inside the chambers the question was: Where is Angela? When the judge asked if anyone knew the whereabouts of Angela everybody answered negatively except Liao who suggested she might have been abducted.

"Abducted!" And, what leads you to believe someone would abduct her?" the judge asked.

Liao replied that he had reason to think one of the American professors may have taken her away to avoid sentencing.

"But," the judge said with a puzzled look on his face, "the charges have been dropped except for the contempt of court. And I would dismiss that as well."

Liao suggested that while everyone is the room knew about the dismissal of charges, Angela did not know, and more importantly, the American did not know. Further, he emphasized, they probably thought she would be spared serious punishment if she escaped.

The judge replied that this was uncalled for; I know her father; he is a party member; I would not have given her any sentence. Yes, but she and the American did not know this. "What a mess!" the judge reflected. He then asked if there were any charges to make against Angela.

Everyone said, "No."

The judge then commented, "Here are two people on the run because they believe the authorities are after them, yet there are no charges against them?"

Again, everyone unanimously agreed.

"Gentlemen," the judge began, "I feel responsible for this. And, I feel responsible for the daughter of my dear friend. To be on the run might take them into dangerous situations, and I could never forgive myself if something happened to her. What do you have to say, Chief Investigator?"

"Judge," I agree. "They could be in danger for no reason. Even the American who has not actually done anything terribly serious is risking his safety and hers as well."

After a few minutes of silence, the judge came to life to say, "Chief Investigator, there is something about this case important enough to bring a man of your stature here. This court supports your efforts in every way. I ask you to find these people, not for interrogation or arrest but for their own protection and to place a protective veil around them so no harm will befall them. They are not to know this; let them continue to think they are escaping. Watch over them, please, to keep them from danger. We have no reason to apprehend them. Use your judgment. Will you accept this assignment as being reasonable?"

"Yes," Liao responded, "I believe it is reasonable. Angela must be protected and the American also as he is a guest in our country. We will find them, judge, and I will report our progress directly to you."

THE DRAGNET

Liao immediately put out orders to Changsha police to check all airports, bus stations, and train stations for the disappearing couple. They also alerted checkpoints at major highways. After a few hours it was apparent the missing couple was either in hiding or had already left. Chan checked the arrival time of Thomas's plane and found it arrived Friday evening. Liao and Chan decided they had at least two days headstart to leaving the country. But, there were no records of them using regular transportation.

This was going to be a greater challenge than Liao and Chan first believed. They took time to think about options of leaving town. Liao asked Chan how did they stop contraband from coming into the country? Do we check the usual transportation routes? No. We look at the unusual transportation because the usual systems have records and checkpoints. For example, a couple of donkeys or horses might slip through to bring something inside the country; why not use the same kind of system to take something out of the country?

Chan asked, "Do you think they are capable of obtaining horses and riding them across country?"

"At this point we should not rule anything out. Angela must know Changsha fairly well, but how well did Thomas know the city, where did he often go?"

"The students walked with the teachers somewhere almost every night, according to court testimony."

"We can retrace their routes. They left the college and walked the winding streets to where? They would go to the 'Japanese store', McDonalds, the water show, the street with the bumps to walk on. Where did Angela say they went on these walks?"

Chan recalled, "She mentioned dancing at the Xiang Park a few times."

They went to the concrete dancing area along the Xiang and looked at the trees, the concrete pillars, and Liao asked," Where is this? Where could they go from here without at least bicycles or a car?" At that moment a boat docking at the pier attracted their attention. They walked to the wall along the river and looked at the Xiang. In a few minutes another boat coughed to life and backed into the river and turned downstream. Liao turned to Chan, put his hand on his shoulder and asked, "Is there not some saying that there is nobody blinder than those who refuse to see?" In a rare mood of closeness, Liao asked Chan, "What do you see?"

Chan looked again and said very slowly, "I see a boat going downstream."

"Repeat!"

"I see a boat going down the river!"

"It is the river!" yelled Liao. "It is the river!" It all fits. They danced along the river, they knew about the boats, and you know about the problem of keeping contraband from coming into the country on the rivers. Why not take something out of the country on the rivers? We would not check boats going out; we check those coming into the country."

Chan asked, "Where are they going?"

"Where can they go? The Xiang empties into Dongting Lake along with the Yangtze, Zi, Yuan, and the Li Rivers. Only one river empties out of the Dongting: the Yangtze! The Yangtze passes Shanghai into the East China Sea. And, what is in Shanghai? Ocean going freighters. They are going to board a freighter that is going to, probably, the United States. We have them, Chan!"

"That is funny," said Chan, "I do not see them!"

"Come on, donkey breathe, we have work to do! We will contact the river patrol and get their opinions about boat traffic," Liao said with enthusiasm. Chan smiled for he could tell his boss was now in his good mood again. They used the helicopter to go to Dongting Lake because after two days or more a boat from Changsha would be close or would have already arrived at the lake.

Tuesday morning, they met with the local river patrol, explained the situation, and asked their advice. The patrol began to estimate how far a boat would have come in two or three days. They concluded the boat must have surely reached Dongting, but where would they be for Dongting Lake is China's second largest lake? The patrol further advised the place to find them is when they leave Dongting on the Yangtze and/or between the lake and the Three Gorges Dam. And, specifically, they mentioned the staircase locks that bypass the dam; for sure you could apprehend them in the locks.

"Thanks," Liao said, "but we do not know the boat or what kind of boat to look for."

The patrol again advised that it might be boat behavior that would help them as much as the looks of the boat itself. For example, a run- down boat that is moving a little too fast for its looks would be suspicious. Also, if the boat is moving straight down the river as though it is in a hurry would also be suspect. After watching the boats a feeling develops about them.

Liao asked if they could spare a man to go with them to watch the boats.

"Sure, it will be our pleasure."

The patrol officer who went with Liao and Chan calculated how far a boat might have come. Even smuggling boats have to stop for some rest and fuel. He calculated a position on the Yangtze that a boat could not have come even if they took no break. He suggested they start their watch a little before that position; therefore, the boat may have passed the first point but could not have gone through the second point.

Liao was pleased. They loaded some equipment, binoculars and an inflatable patrol boat. The helicopter now had pontoons so they could set down in the river. Also, the patrol officer said with a smile that they already knew suspicious captains up and down the Yangtze. As they got to the selected spot in the river, the pilot flew the helicopter slowly and low so they could scan the boats. The patrol officer helped when he pointed out a boat that was obviously a pleasure craft. Another had a crew making repairs. Yet another was wandering aimlessly. He spotted a suspicious looking boat and pointed it out.

"We need to go in for a closer look," said the patrol officer.

The pilot circled the boat, and the captain waved and a couple of crew members come on deck and waved. Not our boat in the opinion of the patrol officer.

And so, it went until about dark and they decided to call it a day and to start at first light the next day. The patrol officer said, "You fellows are becoming good spotters. We will adjust the distance, set a new point on the river, and start in the morning. Tomorrow we will find them!"

The next morning, they had a hit instantly. But, after circling the boat and asking the people on board to show themselves it was not the right one. Shortly after they noticed another boat in some disrepair that was moving faster and straight.

"Look at that one!" said the patrol officer. All three agreed it deserved a closer look. When they asked for crew members, the captain shook his head and pointed to himself.

"We need to stop him," said the patrol officer.

The helicopter landed. Liao instructed Chan to take his sidearm, a radio, and to "look mean and be mean." The patrol officer hailed the captain to heave to; the captain complied, and they tied the patrol boat to the discrepant looking boat. Chan asked permission to board, and the captain waved him on. Chan then asked questions: Where did you start your trip? Who is on board? Where are you going? What are you hauling? May I see your papers?

"There is only my wife. We are empty." Chan said, "I do not believe you, and I am searching the boat!"

The captain began to protest loudly until Chan drew his pistol and told him and his wife to stand on deck, to be quiet, and to not move. Then a movement in the darkness of the boat caught Chan's eye, and he directed his pistol in that direction. Angela appeared as out of a misty darkness and asked, "Are you looking for me?"

Chan stood there and let his eyes adjust to the darkness of the interior of the boat and to give him time to react to Angela's appearance. He was not sure if she recognized him or not. He told her to stand on deck with the captain and his wife. He did not know what to do now that he had the three of them standing on deck. He did not holster his sidearm because he did not trust the grizzly looking captain. He turned on his radio to be in contact with Liao who was watching with binoculars from the helicopter. Liao suggested he question Angela why she was on this tub of a boat.

Chan asked, "Is your name Angela?"

"Yes."

"Are you here of your own free will? Are you being held captive?"

"No, I am here freely," she said.

"Then what are you doing on this boat on the Yangtze River?"

Angela replied, "I wanted to take a boat ride to Shanghai."

"Angela," Chan continued, "you missed your court date on Monday. Why did you not call the court to tell them you could not make it? And, why could this trip not have waited a few days? Did anyone abduct you in Changsha and force you onto this boat?"

"I am sorry, but nobody abducted me," Angela said.

Liao commented into Chan's earpiece, "Drop the questions! She does not want to tell the whole truth; she is afraid you are going to take her back. However, pull that captain off onto the patrol boat, let the patrol boat drift away from his boat, and scare the crap out of him for taking Angela on this trip. Accuse him of trafficking in white slavery; threaten to feed him to the fish."

Chan told the captain, "Please come with me. We have more business with you." When they were out of listening distance from the captain's boat, Chan accused him of selling Angela to a white slaver! The captain's eyes bulged as fear built up inside him. He protested that she rented the boat. Chan menaced him with his pistol and told him that if Angela said one word that she was there against her will, he would shoot him on the spot. The captain sat down and was shaking.

Chan then said, "Okay! Your next job, captain, is to guarantee her safety to Shanghai. Put this protective flag on your flagpole and wait for us to contact you in Shanghai. This flag will be your identification; do not remove it or we will find you and it will not be pretty. And, captain, we will be watching your progress and do not be hard to find. Do you understand?"

The captain looked relieved and said, "Yes, sir."

"And, captain, one more thing," Chan continued, "nobody on the boat is to know about this protective custody. Do you understand that as well?"

"Yes, sir. I tell nobody."

Chan and the captain got back onto the boat. Chan looked directly into Angela's eyes and apologized for the inconvenience and wished her a pleasant trip and he smiled and gave her a brief salute. She did not indicate she recognized him from the trial, but Chan was positive she did.

When Chan and the patrol officer got back to the helicopter and the gear was secured, the helicopter lifted and Liao looked at Chan and said, "I guess I will not have to take you back to the honor guard after all."

ON TO SHANGHAI

When the helicopter was out of sight, Jack emerged from the lower levels of the cabin and asked, "What was that all about?" The captain was semi-mute and said it was a routine stop and check on the boat. "It seemed like a lot of talking going on for a routine check," said Jack.

"Nothing more, nothing," the captain said.

Angela told Jack that the officer was the same one in the courtroom and that he knew her by sight.

"Why did he not take you into custody?" Jack asked.

"I do not know. I have wondered the same thing. He had some private words with the captain but I could not hear them. When the captain came back, he looked like he had seen a ghost!" Both of them commented that the captain had been very quiet.

Jack said, "We can enjoy the boat ride and the view. Soon we will have to pass Three Gorges Dam which is probably the largest dam in the world, and we will have to go through those 'staircase locks' to get past it. Do you think this old tub can handle it?"

"I wonder what our captain friend does in the real world with this old boat that has so much power?" Jack asked.

Angela laughed, "I do not want to know the captain's source of income. His job is to get us to Shanghai."

Jack found a couple of comfortable deck chairs and a small table and set them up on the bow of the boat so they could sit and watch the river and scenery. He found something to drink in the galley and mixed some mild cocktails. As they had settled into their comfortable reclining chairs, a helicopter crossed the boat; they thought it odd that the captain stepped to the deck and gave it a half-hearted wave and salute. They commented that maybe the captain did not want to be stopped again, and both of them had a big laugh at the thought of the captain's discomfort the first time.

The trip continued without incident. They went through the staircase locks and Jack wondered, "Is there not a ghost town, Fengdu, near here? And, what about that bridge called "Nothing to be Done Bridge?"

"Yes, they are around here but we would take too much time to visit them."

They almost lost track of days and time. Jack's comment was that this Yangtze is a long river.

"About 4,000 miles plus or minus," Angela said.

"No wonder we are still chugging along."

For diversion, Jack took a little time at the wheel every day. The captain told him to watch out for those red buoys. Also, Jack had to see the diesel engine and watch it run. Then he and Angela had drinks and sat on the bow and watched for the daily helicopter and laughed every time the captain stepped out on the deck.

In time, the Yangtze changed which indicated they were getting closer to Shanghai. The daily helicopter circled this time and headed south presumably toward the city. At day's end the captain pulled into a marina. He invited them to dinner at a good restaurant. Also, he offered them one hour to shop for needed items, left his wife with them, and disappeared.

"I wonder why he left his wife with us?" asked Jack.

"Probably so we would not run away. Have you paid him everything you owe him?" Angela laughed.

"No."

After one hour, Hogjowl returned and looked pleased with himself. He offered to return to the boat unless they needed more time.

When they got back to the boat, the captain offered a good wine for an after-dinner drink. Then he broke the good news. He told Angela and Jack he had obtained passage on the "Teresa Ann", a freighter that was headed for Los Angeles.

Angela suspiciously said, "We did not ask you to do that!" "Yes, yes, I know," said the captain, "but when the patrol officer and I talked, I asked him if it was possible to book passage on a freighter, and he said, "Of course, if the freighter has room and everybody clears customs."

They have a customs agent on board freighters so I thought it would be quicker and easier to book it immediately then we can go to the "Teresa Ann", tie up, and you can walk up the stairs and, "There you are!"

THE VOYAGE

Around noon the next day, the captain tied up his boat to the Teresa Ann. He led the way up the stairs and said something to the officer on deck. When Jack and Angela got up to the deck, the officer smiled, stamped their luggage, and gave them pieces of paper with a few regulations and the time and location of their meals. They were to eat with the Teresa Ann captain and the other passengers. He also had a member of the crew help them with their little bit of luggage and show them to their cabin.

Jack had already settled up with Hogjowl and they said good-by to him. He was in a hurry to depart.

Angela and Jack later commented about how easy it was to board the freighter. "He never even asked our names or asked for any passports," Jack said.

"Yes, apparently the captain took care of that for us. And, this is a freighter, not a big airport and we do not look like terrorists," Angela laughed.

The dinner guests met promptly at 6:00 pm with the captain who welcomed them. He also bragged about their meal service and said they would try to accommodate individual requests for special meals. Everybody introduced themselves around the table; the captain enjoyed meeting everyone personally. None of the guests attracted any attention except for one Chinese gentleman who dressed casually and looked as though he should be wearing a suit and tie. His name,

Liao, nor his occupation as a financial advisor to a brokerage firm meant anything in this crowd of people.

He and Jack sat across from each other during the meal and exchanged small talk. Jack complimented him on his use of English. After the meal their conversation picked up a little as the food service offered after-dinner drinks. Liao mentioned he remembered Jack was a teacher. They labored through the usual questions about what do you teach and where do you teach. Then Liao ended by saying, "I have thought I would like to teach when I retire."

Jack responded, "Yes, many businessmen say that is what they want to do after they have made their big bucks."

Liao obviously wanted to direct the conversation to more serious issues when he asked Jack what was his impression of China. Jack who was always so free with his comments became cautious because he believed Liao to be well-educated and he did not want to make any foolish statements. He began with the very safe topic of change; change is evident everywhere; the building cranes in the cities, the new airports, the highways, and the schools and universities. "It is clear the Chinese government is investing heavily in the infrastructure and into education for its citizens," Jack concluded.

Liao said, "You know so much about us." Jack did not take the bait, "No, not really. It is casual observation. It is easy to see the people are living a good life with cars, clothes, and celebrating foreign holidays like Valentine's Day and even Christmas. It is an invasion of American culture," and he laughed and said, "The Chinese have discovered our holidays can be fun!"

Liao also laughed, "It is so true. American holidays are fun and Chinese love to enjoy them." To himself Liao thought Jack was being careful about his comments because he did not know him well enough to open up except to give off-the-cuff answers. He thought he might loosen him up a little in the evening.

"Please forgive me," Liao continued, "Are you the couple who came down the Yangtze on some sort of fisherman's boat?"

"Yes."

"You must be tired," said Liao, "and I think I will go to bed after a turn on the deck. Would you and your friend, Angela, is it, like to join me in a brief walk?"

"Yes, we would," said Jack with enthusiasm.

As they walked onto the deck, Liao addressed Angela and asked, "Are you two not an odd couple—a Chinese woman and an American man?" Angela reacted, "No, not really. A truly odd couple would be a Chinese man and an American woman."

"Oh, and why is that?"

Angela blurted out, "Think about it, sir, with a smaller Chinese man and a larger American woman when they would stand toe-to-toe, his nose would be in her flower and if they were nose-to-nose his toe would be in her flower!"

Moments of silence followed until Jack's astonished comment, "Angela!"

Liao doubled up laughing, "You explained it very simply, Angela," He laughed some more and fought the urge to hug her for he had gotten to know her during the trial and now for her to tell a joke like this!

He asked for them to look at the Shanghai Harbor. Look at those container ships. Look at the harbor traffic. Years before China became an independent nation, all this would be foreign. Foreigners, no offense Jack, were sucking the life blood out of China.

Jack intervened to ask, "What about the open-door policy?"

"Ah," Liao smiled, "now the historian comes out of the closet. You know, Jack, the Americans were not here, but they wanted to be here." He continued his comments and said, "This is new China. We are growing economically, culturally, and also politically. We cannot keep the new ideas of the world out of China. We must select and grow with them. Historically, we rejected everything, now we must embrace most things."

Jack asked, "And, you talk about these things and you are a financial broker?" Liao waxed eloquently, "That is the beauty of the new China, Jack. We study other peoples' histories in their own language. For example, in the Changsha Bi-Lingual School the students study your country's history in English with Chinese teachers speaking English. That is cultural power. Do you not like that, Jack?"

"I guess so," said Jack, "but it sounds like a little too much cultural power."

"But, Jack," Liao persisted, "this is not for domination, this is for enrichment and do not forget, it is in English, your language. The genie is out of the lamp; it is not possible to go back; we can only go forward."

The three of them continued their walk on deck.

Mostly Liao pointed out many places in Shanghai and talked of its history. They became cozy except that Jack fumed inwardly and thought Liao should become a tourist guide. When they said good evening Liao could not resist giving Angela a hug, and she hugged him in return. He and Jack shook hands.

When Jack and Angela were in their cabin, Jack began to assess Liao, "He knows too much to be in finance."

"Oh," Angela countered, "somebody would think you were jealous. Do you not like him?"

"That is just it," Jack said, "I like him too much. I do not like financial guys."

Everybody had their thoughts that evening. Liao turned over in his mind the events of the past few days. He wondered what had actually happened at the school; what did happen to Angela. It might be best not to know, and when his vision of the headmaster came to mind, he was sure that it was best not to know. And, then twit Jack who was not actually a twit, but why did he not stay in the states. We handle our own problems. He knew the answer to that question after he got to know Angela. Then he thought about the passport; we let him come into the country and as of now almost out of the country on an illegal use of a passport! Will he later think he made fools of us when all along we knew about it? The safety of Angela is priority; we have protected both of them from harm, and we will lose one of our finest young teachers when Angela leaves. He agonized to himself what good it would do to tell them that they knew about all of this, put them in jail, and have a real trial. Nothing would be gained. He believed he had done the wisest thing in this strange set of circumstances and went to sleep.

The crowd was jovial at breakfast. They genuinely enjoyed their food except for Liao. When the cook came in to see how everyone liked their individually prepared meals, Liao told him he was not satisfied. The cook told him that his request required too much time and he ended up by saying, "You no likee, you go hellie." Everybody got a big laugh out of that famous Chinese sign in front of the laundry in San Francisco.

When the Teresa Ann left the pier, moved through the harbor, and headed for deep water, Liao knew his work was over. He felt good that he had protected Angela from any potential harm; he contacted the judge; the judge would happily tell his old friend, her father, that she was all right. They knew she would be back; she was Chinese. Liao contacted also Chan to tell him to fly out to sea to board an incoming ship and instruct the captain to make a ship- to-ship transfer of a passenger at sea and he would come back to shore on the incoming ship. The captains would arrange the time.

The transfer was set for around 10:00pm. Liao was ready and waiting as the roundabout boat approached and he smelled the sort of pastry he had ordered for breakfast. As the boat tied up to the freighter, he felt a tug on his arm; he turned to look into Angela's eyes. She handed him a bag of warm, freshly baked pastries and leaned in to kiss him on his cheek. He looked at her and in a rare moment was at a loss for words. Then he walked down the stairs to the transfer boat. When he got onto the boat, Chan flashed a light on Angela and yelled her name a couple of times. As the boat turned toward the freighter, both Liao and Chan looked at Angela and yelled her name; she waved with both arms. They looked at her until Liao and Chan disappeared on the other ship.

Liao said to Chan, "She knows."

"Knows what?" Chan asked.

"Knows about us."

"When do you think she first knew something?" Chan asked.

"On the boat on the Yangtze when you did not take her off it. And also, when she saw me on the freighter, she suspected something," Liao smiled.

THE U.S. OF A

Jack was looking forward to talking with Liao at breakfast but he was not there. When Jack figured he was missing, he asked the captain what had happened to him. The captain explained that urgent business required he return to Shanghai. Jack muttered under his breath, "He must have had to make some million-dollar financial deal?"

"Now, do not be sarcastic, Jack," Angela said.

"Well, hell, who am I going to talk to?"

"You could talk to me," Angela said teasingly.

"You know what I mean," Jack replied.

Life on board the deep-water freighter became routine. Jack and Angela ate their meals together with the other guests; they strolled the deck, sat in the deck chairs, watched movies at night, played some poker with a few of the guests, and whiled away the time.

Excitement picked up when the captain announced shore lights. Everybody gathered on deck to glimpse a few far and remote lights. Jack and Angela had their few belongings ready to go in an instant. Jack had already made arrangements with the captain to run them ashore in a small boat; the captain had already been told two passengers might want off before the ship docked. Jack did not ask questions.

It was time to walk down the stairs and board the small boat. When the boat left the freighter, the pilot told them the jumping off place was a popular hangout for teenagers to gather at night, build fires, to drink, and to generally party. Also, it was not far from a highway and a small town.

As their feet touched the ground, they were a bit unsteady but that soon passed. Then they walked toward what they hoped was a town or at least some people. But the beach areas were empty; they heard no noise; there was no car traffic. They continued to walk. They entered the town but it appeared to be completely empty of people. Jack wondered what was happening for this seemed like something out of the "Twilight Zone." They walked on; suddenly from out of darkness a police car came alongside them and an officer flashed a light on them.

The nearest officer asked, "Hey, Jack, what are you doing out here?"

Jack responded, "How did you know my name?"

The officer got out of the car, walked up to them, and asked, "Are you getting wise with me?"

"No sir, Jack is my name."

"What are you doing here?"

"We are trying to find our way," Jack replied.

"Where are you going?"

"We do not know because we do not know what there is to go to," said Jack.

"Do you know there is a statewide curfew?" asked the officer.

"No."

"Where have you been to not know about the curfew?"

"China."

"Look, if you are going to get smart with me, I will run you in to the station. You do not look Chinese to me. Did she come from China too?"

Angela piped up and said, "Made in China!"

The officer's eyes popped and his mouth dropped open a little and he said, "Are you sure about that, little missy?" And, he looked at her a little closer as Angela responded in her crisp British accent, "Quite."

Jack asked, "Why is there a statewide curfew?"

The officer explained that numerous protests against President Trump's attacks on California caused the Governor to impose a curfew to stop any potential violence.

Jack continued, "We have no money and are hungry. Will you take us to the police station?"

The officer was exasperated, "You two are a couple of fruitcakes," he concluded, "and I am not wasting my time on you."

"But, we need help," pleaded Jack, "and you are supposed to protect and serve. At least take us to a motel and a place where we can get some food. And, I would like to borrow $100 from you personally, not from you because you are a police officer."

"You are nuts!" the officer laughed, "but nutty enough I am going to take a chance on you."

Jack and Angela piled into the police car, the officer loaned him $100, and he took them to a modest motel. And, he said, "I will be here 9:00am in the morning to get my $100."

As Jack and Angela walked away from the police car, they waved good-by to the officers and thanked them. Then Jack said to Angela, "Oh, by the way, welcome to the U. S. of A!"

THE WILLIS TOWER BOMB

This just in! Our newsroom reports that law enforcement officials foiled an attempt to detonate a bomb in the Willis Tower, Chicago, Illinois. Information is limited, but it is believed that three or four Chinese immigrants with links to a dissident group in China planned to create an incident in the United States to cause conflict between two governments.

The Chinese government has pledged to assist in the investigation in all ways possible.

More news will be made available as soon as possible.

JACK'S FARM HOUSE

It was a beautiful, sunny morning at Jack's farm in northern Illinois. The sun was just breaking above the horizon and streaming into the bedroom. It was nature's alarm clock telling him it was time to get out of bed and to get moving. He was already awake but liked to watch the sunlight pour through the windows into the room.

A knocking at the door interrupted this tranquil scene. Jack hurriedly put on some clothes and walked down the short hallway through the kitchen and the utility room to answer the door. On the way he glanced out the kitchen windows to see two police cars parked in the driveway. As he looked out the window next to the door, he saw one uniformed officer and one other person, presumably a plains clothes officer, standing on the porch.

Jack opened the door slowly and asked, "May I help you?"

The plains clothes person answered with a question, "Is this the residence of Jack Thomas and are you Jack Thomas?"

Yes and yes.

"I am Chief Detective Donald Matthews of the Illinois State Police, Northern District and this is Sergeant Larry Jessup of the Illinois State Police, post # 9. We have urgent business with you; may we come in?"

Jack looked at him with a puzzled look on his face for a moment or two and said, "Please, my house is always open to law enforcement people. There is little to offer you at this time but in a few minutes there will be some hot coffee and something to eat."

Matthews and Jessup walked into the kitchen, and Jack noted two other state police positioned at strategic places around the house.

Matthews asked, "Would it be all right, Jack, if we took seats at the table so I can briefly tell you why we are here?"

"Of course, that is a good idea as I am curious why you would have any interest in me," replied Jack.

Matthews continued, "Jack I can only tell you brief details but we are here to escort you into the city (Chicago), not under duress or under arrest but only if you freely and willingly go with us." Jack looked even more confused and asked, "Do I actually have a choice?"

"Yes, you do," Matthews replied, "if you tell me right now you do not want to go, we will not say another word and we will leave. Do you trust us to act in your best interest? We will escort you to the city, provide for your lodging, and your expenses."

"What is this all about?" Jack asked cautiously.

Matthews answered that he could only give him the barest of information but said he would be told when it was appropriate. That is why you must trust us at this time.

Jack said, "If the Illinois State Police cannot be trusted, who can be? Let's get moving."

Matthews smiled at that and said, "That is what I hoped you would say. From this time forward you are under the protective custody of the Illinois State Police. Now, will you pack a small overnight bag with change of clothes, your toiletries, and other needs, take your usual morning shower and shave, and we will fix breakfast for you."

Jack threw back over his shoulder as he was walking toward the bedroom, "How do you know I shower and shave and how do you know how I like breakfast? Oh, and while you are at it, fix something for the rest of your guys as well; I do not want to eat in front of anyone. You know I have guns in my bedroom!"

"We know you are a real desperado, Jack. This is only the tip of the iceberg of what we know about you," Matthews replied.

In about 30 minutes, Jack emerged from the bedroom with a fresh shave and his favorite travel bag. And, there was a delicious aroma of fresh coffee and freshly cooked bacon in the air. Except for one lookout, the troopers (big boys, Jack thought) prepared to eat; they served Jack and Matthews and gathered around the table. Jack commented, "How did you get such delicious food out of this kitchen?"

That provoked a few smiles out of what were pretty serious fellows, "We just worked at it."

When the meal and small talk were almost over, Matthews hit a number on his phone and said, "We are ready in five minutes. Time to brush your teeth, Jack, we will leave the place as nobody has been here. Saddle up, boys, we are ready."

In exactly five minutes, a state police helicopter landed in the backyard as Jack and Matthews exited the house. Jack wowed over that and said, "You do not waste time do you?"

Matthews turned serious, "No, Jack, we don't and especially in this situation. Do you want to back out?"

"Are you kidding?' Jack laughed, "All the soybeans in China could not keep me off that 'copter'".

Matthews briefed Jack as the helicopter got off the ground, "I know you have questions but in 15 minutes you will meet some people who will tell you more. Thank you for your trust in the Illinois State Police and, Jack, I will be with you as long as necessary and will help you through what is to follow."

Jack looked down at his farm—the house, barn, pond—as it very quickly became all flat and indistinguishable and wondered, just wondered what had brought all this to happen.

As Matthews said, the helicopter landed in a little under 15 minutes at the 'copter' pad at the University of Chicago Medical Center. Jack's first reaction as he looked at Matthews was, "What the hell…?"

Matthews responded with a hand on Jack's back, "Very soon, very soon, just hold on a few more minutes."

A little mobile cart whisked them to the appropriate building as a couple of hospital security people met them and escorted them to room 4147 in the intensive care unit.

As they approached the door to room 4147, Matthews cautioned Jack again to take it easy and to expect the unexpected as he pushed the door open for him to enter the room.

Jack cautiously walked through the door and looked dazed as he saw a small group of people—a female physician, a Chinese dressed sharply in military uniform, three other well-dressed men—one of whom approached him with outstretched hand and said, "Hello, Jack."

Jack mechanically took the outstretched hand as he looked directly into the eyes of the man in front of him and after he got over the initial shock said, "YOU! You again! I thought we had finished with you on the ship."

Chief Investigator Liao said very quietly, "No, Jack, we are only beginning!"

ON THE WAY HOME

"Jack, you silly man, are you really broke and have no money as you told that police officer?" Angela asked.

"No, I am not completely broke but that ship was not overly generous as I converted the Yuan into US greenbacks," Jack replied.

"Then why," Angela wondered, "did you go through all that process with the officer to have him take us to the police station and to borrow money from him to pay for a motel?"

"Let's look at our situation. Neither of us cleared U. S. Customs and in your case you are a Chinese national in the United States illegally. And, that makes you an illegal alien," Jack answered.

At this Angela said, "Oh, yes, I am a terrible person; I am a fugitive from justice in my home country and an illegal alien in your country. What else can happen?"

"Exactly," said Jack, "you are in a mell of a hess (Jack likes Spoonerisms) especially if that cop had been more inquisitive. What better way to distract him than to pretend to be something far-fetched as coming from China. Your comment about being made in China further convinced him we were two strange birds rather than 'international criminals.' Plus, I always did want to ask some police officer to take me to the station for help. You saw how he waffled. Also, immigration is a really touchy issue in the United States now. If he had asked for identification, he might have discovered our deception. So, a little blarney can go a long way; you saw how quickly he decided we were harmless."

Angela did not miss the blarney comment and asked what it meant. Jack explained about the Blarney Stone in the Irish castle that people would climb and lean out from the wall to pull themselves up a bit to kiss the "blarney stone" to get the gift of gab. She asked if this was like BS and 'blowing hot air.'

"Yes," Jack said, "you have the idea."

"Back to our situation. We need to put some distance between us, those police officers, Los Angeles, and blend as tourists," Jack emphasized.

"And, just how are we doing that since you are so broke?" mocked Angela.

"Okay, miss smarty pants, first, we get a car at a car rental; secondly, we get some extra cash at an ATM; thirdly, we pick up a Rand McNally road map, and we will be on our way."

"No GPS?"

"No, I prefer an old-fashioned map," said Jack.

"How will we know where to go?" Angela persisted.

"Because you will be the map reader and navigator," said Jack.

"Surely, you are kidding," a surprised Angela commented.

"Oh, do not worry; we have only about 2,500 miles to cover before we get home," laughed Jack.

"Why not fly?" asked Angela.

Jack responded seriously, "Angela, you have no U. S. driver's license for a picture identification; you have no proof of entering this country; your Chinese passport is actually proof of illegal entry as there would be no custom's stamp and date of entry. Trust me! We have to avoid certain things like police officers, law enforcement people of any kind who might be nosy about your passport. And, on a brighter side we will see some of our country's most beautiful places on the way."

"Well, let's hit the road, Jack, and don't look back," both laughed at the reference to a popular song.

The next morning after Jack paid the police officer the $100 he had borrowed, he and Angela got a rental car, some cash, and a map and prepared to start their long journey. Jack commented that once they got out of Los Angeles everything would smooth out. He showed Angela where they were and showed her the final destination in northern Illinois. She asked if they would ever get there.

"Yes, we will get there if the navigator reads the map correctly. Here we are in Los Angeles; we want to get on Interstate 15 to get out of California; Interstate 15 will take us through Las Vegas, Nevada; in fact, Interstate 15 will take us to Montana, but just before we get to Montana, we will swing right on Highway #20 at Idaho Falls. Do you see how this works," asked Jack.

"Of course," she replied, "but would a GPS not be simpler to use?"

"Maybe, but I do not like a GPS with somebody telling you where to go," commented Jack.

"Now, the real reason emerges; you do not want a boss telling you where to drive."

Jack replied, "Yes, that may be it, especially a robot on the other end, a mechanical person."

They drove for quite some time and finally got out of California.

Angela piped up to say, "It looks like we are missing a lot of things to see by staying on this one Highway Interstate 15."

"Yes, but I am taking you to the most beautiful place in the whole of the United States, and we do not have that much time to look at all the places on the way," was Jack's answer.

"But, what if I want to see some of these other things?" she persisted.

"They are not going anywhere; they will still be there in years to come," said Jack.

"I want to see them now," said Angela, "and since we are so close why not take the time?"

"Because, as I have explained, we do not have the time to wander around in California; it is such a big state," Jack answered.

"You just want to be the boss," complained Angela.

"What? Are you fussing at me?" said a somewhat irritated Jack, "I am not so sure whoever taught you English did the world a favor."

"Really. So, now I am a pest to you? If you want me to be the navigator, I can decide where we go," argued Angela.

"No, because I am the captain and the navigator navigates to the captain's destination," Jack responded.

"Maybe we can do something about who the captain is," Angela answered. "We will see who the captain is if you keep fussing because I will pinch one or two of your titties," threatened Jack.

"Wowowo, here they are, big boy," Angela twisted around in the seat to thrust her chest forward and toward Jack, "come and get them," she taunted him," I will even take off my harness to make it easier for you to get to them, although you have never had any problem finding them."

"You shameless hussy; you know I have to keep my eyes on the road rather than look at your prominent titties," Jack replied.

Angela started laughing as she waved her "harness" in front of Jack's face.

Jack was about to respond when a Utah State Police car came up behind them with lights flashing but without the siren. Jack quickly said, "Look what you have done; it is illegal to take your bra off while driving because of such dangerous distractions."

Angela looked at him with a bit of concern.

As the state trooper approached the car, Jack rolled the door window down. The trooper looked inside at Jack and Angela and asked, "May I see your identification, car registration, and insurance, please. And, I would like identification for both of you," he added.

Jack gave him his Illinois driver's license, the car rental papers, and Angela handed over her Chinese national identification card and her Chinese driver's license. Neither Jack nor Angela said a word. The trooper thanked them and said, "I will be back shortly."

"See what your little stunt caused," said Jack.

"You are just being ridiculous," she said, "and are wanting to pick on me."

"Yeah. What if he asks for your passport?" replied an alarmed Jack, "that would be a feather in his cap if he apprehended a desperate fugitive from justice who had entered the United States illegally. Trump (the President) would give him a medal."

After a few tense moments, both troopers returned. The first one gave Jack his driver's license and papers back and asked both of them to exit the car. The second trooper asked Angela to return to the police car with him. She did. When they got inside the car, the trooper got on his phone to dispatch and asked if they could connect the phone call. Yes! He then handed her the phone and said, "They are on the line, push this little button to talk and let up on it to receive." Angela nodded her head yes. The trooper then said, "I will leave the car so you can have privacy; signal thumbs up when you are finished!" And, he gave her a thumbs up when he left.

After the trooper left, Angela spoke into the microphone, "Hello, this is Angela."

"Hello. How are you doing?" the voice at the other end asked.

"We are fine and moving pretty fast. He wants to get to Yellowstone National Park," she replied.

"Did the two Los Angeles cops find you?"

"Yes. That was funny," she answered. "Okay. I will be in Chicago before you get there. Expect another contact before you get to your destination to check on you. We are working to get everything ready for you in Chicago. Take care! Enjoy the park! Over and out."

"Yes. Will do. Thanks. Will talk later," and with that comment she gave a thumbs up to the officer who returned to the police car.

As the second trooper joined Jack and the first one while Angela was on the phone, he heard conversations about Mormons in Utah. The first trooper said to him that they had a wild one on their hands with Jack because as he explained he asked Jack if he had a gun and he replied that he had a grease gun. You know, a grease gun to grease farm implements. The second trooper said, "Isn't that just too cute."

Jack shrugged and laughed when he said, "I never had the chance to tell a police officer that until you two guys. I bet you Utah fellows know all about greasing farm equipment." They all had a little chuckle."

The second trooper said to Jack, "Your friend is filling out some papers; she should be finished in a few minutes." He kept a close eye on the patrol car; suddenly he went back and retrieved Angela. When they got back into the car, the troopers offered them snacks, something to drink and explained that this was a "courtesy stop" compliments of the State of Utah to welcome out-of-state travelers and to have them rest and to stretch their legs as a safety precaution. The troopers then wished them good traveling with the parting words of the second trooper to Jack even though he was looking and smiling at Angela, "Do not let 'Miss China' drive on her driver's license because it will not work here!" They parted company with handshakes all around.

Jack took off cautiously and easily. Soon the patrol car roared by them; the troopers waved; and then they turned on an emergency crossover through the median and flew off in the opposite direction.

After a moment, Angela commented, "Look at them showing off."

Jack said, "All for your benefit."

"What do you mean?" asked Angela.

"Don't pretend you do not know you are a 'hottie' and with all that 'special treatment' that guy gave you in the police car! Did he ask you where your bra was?"

Angela's response was to cuddle up to Jack, to put one arm through his, and to lay her head on his shoulder and to purr, "Jack, you are so easy."

"My Captain, My Captain, I will go with you anywhere you want with no fuss, no bother," she said as she kissed him on his neck and laughed, "Do you not know that by now?"

After spending the night at Idaho Falls (not much before or after) and reviewing the route for the day which would include entering Yellowstone National Park at the western entrance, Jack and Angela ate breakfast, filled the car with fuel, and took off.

The previous day they had stopped at an Indian trading post, and Jack bought Angela an Indian bandanna she could tie around her head to help control her hair. She asked Jack why these people were so friendly to her and always smiling at her. Jack laughed and said, "Because they think you are an Indian."

"An Indian!"

"Yes, an Indian! These people are descendants of your ancestors, you know, ancient peoples some of whom migrated here thousands of years ago!"

Angela may have hoped surely not another history lesson, but Jack kept it very short as he explained that being taken for an Indian would divert attention away from being Chinese.

She thought about this briefly and then laughed as she said, "I see; I understand; I can be one of the Ten Little Indians."

Yes.

"You are a funny man," she concluded.

The western entrance to Yellowstone National Park loomed in the distance. Jack presented his national park pass (He called it the 'golden Eagle pass') at the checkpoint and they waved him through.

Angela said, "You must be a man of importance to just go on through."

"No, it is a lifetime pass for all our national parks. I bought it years ago at the Little Big Horn National Park," Jack explained.

"Now that we are in the park, look carefully for there probably will be buffalo and we might possibly see a bear. But, the highlight of Yellowstone is 'Old Faithful'."

"Old Faithful what?" she asked.

Old Faithful is a geyser, a water spout that blows water into the air at regular and predictable times winter, summer, fall, and spring.

"Will we get wet?"

"No, everyone watches from a distance."

When they got to the geyser the posted predicted time for the eruption was about two hours away. Perfect time! Time to rest, get a bite to eat, and to find a good spot to view the geyser blowing its top. Time seemed to crawl like a "watched pot never boils" but almost exactly on the time predicted "Old Faithful" WAS faithful and began to show off its water performance.

Angela squealed with delight!

After the geyser subsided the next objective was an Indian school in Ashland, Montana. This was the one charity Jack contributed to and he wanted to see the school. When they entered the campus they went to the administration office; the Executive Director, Yellow Arrows, greeted them warmly as Jack has been contributing to the school. Jack asked to see the new heating and air conditioning the school had recently installed. Yellow Arrows was proud to show the new system and described how it was so much better than the old one. It was expensive but it had to be done; it was working fine. Then Jack wanted to see a classroom; the teacher asked Angela if she would tell the kids about her "tribe?" Yes, Angela told them about her tribe or the "Han" in China. The kids were all attentive and then she led them in some songs. Afterwards the kids gathered around her to talk to her and to hug her. Everybody had a good time.

They left the Indian school and continued toward Rapid City, South Dakota, on Highway # 212. After declaring it a day, they pulled over to spend the night, to rest, and to catch up on news. And, the map was pulled out to plan the next day's agenda. The next major objective was to see the Presidents on Mount Rushmore. Except that Jack was not very excited about seeing Teddy Roosevelt for he believed he had done a lot to create a monster when he supported Japan. "And, what did that monster do?" as he continued his tirade against Teddy, "it became a Pit Bull, uncontrollable, and bit the United States in the rear end when it (the Pit Bull) bombed Pearl Harbor. There should be a movement to blast his ugly mug off the mountain!"

"Surely, you are exaggerating," said Angela in a teasing way to tweak Jack even more.

"You think," said Jack, "this Pit Bull did a lot more damage to China, your people, than it did to us, but it fell to us to clean up the mess that we, Teddy, had created. I know what you are trying to do; you want to get me upset but it will not work. The United States had to face the situation that we had created at the turn of the century when we gave Japan the "green light" to do whatever they wanted in Asia. We paid the price; we cleaned up the mess; the world is a lot better off today."

"Yes, Jack, whatever you say, Jack," tweaked Angela.

"Well, that is what I say," said Jack.

As Jack and Angela walked toward the door to go outside to view the four Presidents, a United States Park Ranger stopped them. "Hello, my name is Mark Harris, United States Park Ranger, and may I ask you a few questions?" he asked.

"Sure," said Jack, "but there are no guarantees you will get any answers."

"May I ask your names?"

"Yes," replied Jack.

After a few awkward moments the ranger said, "Well, what are your names?"

"You asked if you could ask our names, and I said yes," Jack replied, "and now you have asked."

"Would you mind telling me your names?" the ranger persisted. "Yes, I do mind. Why do you want our names? Is there any probable cause? What have we done for you to even talk to us?"

"I see. Let me start over. The park service likes to talk to randomly-selected people to welcome them and to get a feeling about the many diverse people who visit our parks," responded the ranger.

"I don't believe you randomly selected us; I believe you have curiosity or suspicions about where I might be from and particularly where my companion with a headband is from and what we might be doing here. How am I doing so far?" he said to the startled ranger.

"Yes, you are pretty much on target. A couple like you raises some suspicion as to citizenship and your presence here. Let me start over again and ask you for your help. We have had problems with people who wear bandannas and we would like to put the suspicions out of our minds. So, will you help us?" the ranger concluded.

Jack looked at him and said, "Only on the condition you recognize our rights under the 4th and 14th Amendments and several court rulings that we do not have to answer any of your questions without probable cause and/or without presence of counsel."

"That is no problem at all. We are on the right side of the law. We would not do anything illegal or the government would pull our badges. Now, will you help us? I can tell already that you are not from around here but probably from the lower Midwest like southern Indiana or southern Illinois or somewhere in that general region," the ranger said.

"And, I can tell immediately that you ARE from around here and that you are probably a Crow Indian," replied Jack.

The ranger looked incredulously at Jack and asked, "How did you know that?"

The reply intrigued the ranger, "First, you are obviously a descendant of American Indians; secondly, the Crow Indians always worked for the United States—from Custer to the present—and, you are the present."

The ranger laughed as he said, "You have passed your citizenship test but may I—and I emphasize—*may* I ask your friend some questions in my office? If we hit a snag, we will call you; you can look through the office window to see what we are doing."

"Angela, it is up to you because you do not have to say a word, and the ranger knows it," a concerned Jack told her.

"It is all right. I have nothing to hide; I have done nothing," said Angela.

Jack's thoughts were racing now as he was saying to himself— nothing except escaping from China, avoiding the court there, and being an illegal alien here. He paced nervously as he kept an eye on the window and thought of her passport and of a sheep being led to the slaughter. He saw them immediately start laughing and wondered what was so funny.

As the ranger escorted Angela into his office and closed the door he offered her a chair and said, "I thought I was never going to get around Clarence Darrow! Your boss told me to tell you 'hello' and to wish you a good time in the park," and then he laughed.

She laughed also and asked if there was any other message for her.

"Yes, in fact, he told me to tell you the next contact would be from a neighbor on the road where Jack's farm is located," and, the ranger added, "thank you for wearing that bandanna because it made it very easy to spot you in the crowds of people." They both laughed.

"Before we go, go through your purse and give me your I.D. and driver's license so I can pretend to be checking on you. That way Jack will think I am interrogating you." She complied.

Then she and the park ranger left the office and both were laughing as Angela told him the story about how she described her "tribe" to the school children. As the three of them came together in the lobby, the ranger said, "Jack, for the trouble and inconvenience on behalf of the United States Park Service, I want to give you a meal voucher that is good at any national park and to thank you for your support of the National Parks Association."

"How do you know my name and my support of the parks?" a still suspicious Jack asked. "I believe Angela mentioned it. And, remember we are here to protect and to serve."

"Yeah, like you guys protected and served poor old General Custer?" was Jack's reply.

"Hey, we did help Custer and, contrary to all stories about it, he took and acted on our advice as well. And, several Crow Indians died in that battle," the ranger was very proud of his ancestry.

"Yes. You are right. Of course, you are right. You probably present programs about that battle," said Jack. At that the ranger beamed and nodded his head.

Jack and Angela thanked him for the meal voucher and shook his hand. When they were out of ear shot, Jack said, "Let's look at the Presidents and get the hell out of here before Chief "Smiling Face" gets other ideas."

"Why have you acted this way?" Angela asked.

"Because that is the way they are. They ask these harmless little questions like where are you from and where are you going to trip you up on details. And, if you answer one of them wrong, they will take you somewhere for more intensive questioning. My behavior was to make me look like some sort of civil rights fanatic to draw attention away from you. Did he ask you for your passport?" Jack ended his tirade.

"No. He asked for my I. D. and a driver's license and where I was from. That was it," she emphasized.

"Just remember that if any law official such as a national park ranger who has similar authority as state police, city police, etc., were to see your passport, it might be all over," Jack labored again to have her understand the consequences of being in the country illegally.

What do you mean? They would detain you and notify immigration that they had an illegal alien.

"I see. I understand," she said somewhat meekly.

"We have been lucky. This makes the third time—those Los Angeles cops, the Utah State Troopers, National Park Rangers— there were opportunities for law officials to discover your passport. I have never been stopped so much before," complained Jack.

They looked at the four Presidents, made some comments, and left the park.

As they got into the car to leave the park, Jack said, "Now, we are in for the long haul home. There are several places we could stop in Iowa, such as the Amanas or Homestead where the Amana Society bought several thousands of acres of prime farm land to start their society or Anamosa, Iowa, where I spent a summer working, or Osage, Iowa, where I spent another summer working but we need to get home as quickly as possible.

"Okay, Captain Jack," Angela retorted.

Jack looked at her, "You are really trying to get under my skin, aren't you?"

"Whatever gave you that idea?" she demurred.

Jack emphasized it was time to burn up highway and to get home. The route would be Interstate 90 to Interstate 35 to Interstate 80. When they got closer to Chicago, they would have to take two-lane highways to get to Jack's farm. Jack talked about a couple of books along the way: BLUE HIGHWAYS, Least Heat Moon, and John Steinbeck, TRAVELS WITH CHARLEY. He mentioned how he had always thought about duplicating a trip much like Steinbeck's across the United States; but he hastened to add that the Interstate Highway System or the Eisenhower Interstate Highway System was one of the wonders of the modern world. And, if a traveler wanted to drive from here to there the quickest way possible, the interstate was the way to go. He added that Ike, while he was in the military, was given an assignment to move his army unit from the east coast to the west coast; it was such a mess, he commented in his memoirs that what this country needs is a better system of roads. When Eisenhower became President, he supported the Interstate Highway Act. Jack also laughed when he described how he worked on the construction of the interstate roads and how that helped put him through college.

"Then he asked if she could see a big hill that the highway cut through?"

"Yes, I can see something as big as that hill."

"Well, I worked one summer helping to move that hill!"

Not much happened until they reached the road where the farm was located. Jack decided to play a trick on Angela, "Let's see if you can recognize the farm from pictures and descriptions?"

Angela replied, "That's ridiculous. You know I have no idea where we are."

"Yeah, but I will stop at a few places to see if you might think it is a place where I might live. For example, what about this place?" Jack had stopped in front of an old dairy farm that had junk farm equipment laying everywhere around the barn and in the barnyard; there were piles of cow manure here and there; the house had not seen paint in years and had no yard, but a weed garden. It was undoubtedly one of the most cluttered, unkempt places in the neighborhood.

"Do you think this is it?" asked Jack. "If this is it, I am out of here as quickly as possible," was Angela's reaction.

Jack laughed and laughed.

The next place he stopped was a beautiful brick house with a concrete driveway, well-groomed yard, and had well-located trees around the house.

"Is this it?"

"This is a beautiful place, but I don't think so."

Jack deliberately and slowly drove past his place to see if there would be a reaction, but said nothing. He heard an "Hmm . . ." He went on, turned around, and started back on the road in the direction they had come.

Angela said, "Oh, come on, Jack, let's stop this silly little game of yours. I bet we have already driven past it."

"And, you are correct, for here it is," he said as he pulled into the driveway and parked the car by the porch."

"I suspected this one when we drove by it, for it is a pretty, big farm house with a red barn and a pond."

"Yes, welcome to the plantation," said Jack.

"What a nice relief after such a long trip," Angela responded. Jack agreed, "It is a good place to call home."

They unloaded the car, put some things away, and put dirty clothes in the laundry. Just as they started to relax, a knock on the door interrupted the routine, "Hello, I am from the house with the big red barn down the road. I have been watching over your place in case some stranger might decide to do something here. We see Jack coming and going, and when he is not here, we keep an eye on things; we have a good unofficial neighborhood watch program.

After introductions, the lady asked Angela if she would help bring some "house-warming" things into the house from her car.

Sure. Once outside the house, the lady said softly, "Everything is ready for you in Chicago. The task force has formed, plans are complete, and it is time for you to go there. Your role is worked out as well. I will pick you up; we will go to my house; a helicopter will take you into the city."

When they had taken drinks, snacks, and other items into the house, the lady asked Angela if she might like to join her and her friends some night for a "ladies' night out"? Both Angela and Jack responded positively to her invitation.

THE TASK FORCE

Dissident and/or insurgent groups in China have limited expression, especially certain ones in the far western provinces who feel China has no right to control them. These groups feel strongly about this and some of them have resorted to violence. Over a period of time feelings can grow stronger to develop into hatred.

The problem intensifies if members of these groups immigrate to another country. China's control of their behavior is weakened and is ineffective. This happened with three Chinese individuals who migrated to Chicago who had ties with the dissident groups. Chinese officials know about these individuals, monitor their communications, and are concerned about their behavior. Chinese authorities contacted the United States Homeland Security and explained their suspicions; United States authorities are appreciative of this kind of information from any country; in this case U.S. authorities invited Chinese law enforcement to come to the United States and to help determine suitable action.

Detective Matthews of the Illinois State Police welcomed the assembled gathering of law enforcement people and read a statement from the Secretary of United States Homeland Security:

Let me say on behalf of Homeland Security and the people of the United States how much we appreciate the concern and cooperation of Chinese authorities who have notified us of a possible threat to our security. It is the objective of every law enforcement officer in this country and of countries abroad to prevent any unlawful act that takes lives and destroys property. I wish this task force every success.

Matthews, ranking member of the task force, continued to welcome law enforcement personnel, especially the Chinese guests, to the task force, "Welcome to our task force and welcome to the United States. Thank you for your help and your concern." He then discussed the problems with a task force and its limitations; for example, he explained how they could not arrest anyone on suspicion; that they can only arrest people after they have done something. We may have suspicions that these individuals are going to commit a conspiracy but we must have at least one act of agreement among them they are going to commit this act; such an act might be trying to recruit someone else into their conspiracy. There must be two or more people involved in this conspiracy. We must be very careful to be able to prove they have committed a conspiracy because we do not want the courts to throw it out for lack of proof. If we wait until they have actually done something, it may be too late with disastrous consequences. So, we have to, in my opinion, lay a trap to allow them to reveal their plans; if they have taken steps toward a disruptive event, we can arrest them. At that point they have done something.

The problem is further compounded as the suspects are Chinese nationals. If American authorities were to approach them, they would abandon their plans momentarily only to plan something in the future. In as much as the Chinese notified us of their suspicions it is only appropriate that they present their ideas about apprehending these suspected individuals.

The Chinese representative now took the podium and presented their plan. Thank you for taking our warnings and suspicions seriously. We are on the same side and are working with common interests: to avoid an incident that could take lives, destroy property, and disrupt relations between our countries. We understand our role to identify and to assist as we are guests in your country, but let me assure you our lack of authority will not dampen our work effort. There is one member of our team not present for she is traveling across country to arrive in Chicago in a few days. She speaks English fluently; her cover story is that she escaped China and is fleeing from authorities, has bad feelings about losing her teaching job, and has entered the United States illegally. She is an illegal alien. With help from the Illinois State Police and Chicago Police Department, thank you very much, we have set up a "sting operation" designed to lure these individuals out of hiding and to cause them to reveal their plans. Also, she is an attractive Chinese woman who will get their attention. She hopefully will be a temptation for them to try to recruit her to their cause; she will be an "ice queen" with ice water in her veins, haughty, and arrogant if and when they contact her. The idea is they will try to impress her with their plans whatever they might be.

Spontaneous questions erupted? How is this going to work? How will she be exposed to them?

Here is the plan. The Chicago Police Department has convinced the owner of the "Country Music Club" to let her sing. Groans of "Oh, my God. The roughest place in town. Chief headquarters for the law breakers in town. And, can she sing?" The Chinese laughed. Exactly. That is why we picked it. She is a law breaker, remember, an illegal alien; as to whether she can sing? I guarantee it. But, it will be nice if a few officers are there as ordinary citizens with family perhaps to enjoy the show; it will be added security and you can judge for yourself about her singing. A few more eyes, a few more undercover police officers, a few more "drinkers" won't hurt a thing. The Chicago PD has the owner "shaking in his boots" so he is on our side also.

Let me describe the "Country Music Club." It has seating capacity of around 250 people; it has a semi-circular elevated stage and has good lighting and sound equipment. There is a dance floor that curves around the stage; there is one entrance and five well-marked exits. The entrance is a short hallway where doormen frisk clients for weapons. Police officers should exercise caution about flaunting badges as that arouses suspicion. The last person clients pass by to get inside is the bouncer who guards the inside entrance of the hallway.

The only person in the club who knows of this plan is the owner. He does not know what we are after but only that a girl is singing. Actually, everybody there would wish us success to catch these suspects because we hope to prevent some tragic event.

We will work on details or problems as they arise. But, so far, everyone in Chicago has been congenial, friendly, and receptive to catching these guys. It does not embarrass me that they are Chinese; law breakers transcend national boundaries; they are evil people who intend to do harm to your country. This task force intends to see that they fail. Thank you for your help and support. With that last comment, Chief Investigator Liao turned the meeting back to Matthews.

In his style of leadership, Matthews said, "Gear up, fellows, make us proud, get in the right frame of mind; with the help of our Chinese friends, we are going to identify and nail these bastards." If there is anyone among us who has reservations about this, let's hear it now. "Shouts of 'no', 'hell, no,' 'let's get them', echoed throughout. One comment emerged, "What about Chan's military uniform? Isn't it about time he ditched that and started to wear regular clothes; those Chinese would spot that a mile away?" Everybody laughed.

Matthews then said, "We need to visit, to talk, and to get to know each other. We are a team; we must be comfortable together."

THE ICE QUEEN

The opening night for the "ice queen" at the Country Music Club finally arrived. Angela dressed modestly in a red sleeveless dress that hugged her neck; it extended slightly below her knees with a short slit—3 to 4 inches—on both legs. The dress concealed, not revealed, her shapely figure; it was not tight but hugged her body. A hush fell over the crowd as she walked onto the stage; the sound effects man had the loud speakers blurt out, "Ladieeeeees and gentlemen, welcome to The Country Music Club the 'Chinese Country Bumpkin,'" in a manner of sound effects often heard at sporting events. There was polite clapping. Angela paused, nodded her head, and began:

He walked into the bar and parked his lanky frame on a tall barstool.

With a long soft Southern drawl said,

I'll just have a glass of anything that's cool.

A bar room girl with hard and knowing eyes slowly looked him up and down.

And she thought, 'I wonder how on earth that country bumpkin found his way to town?' (At this point someone yelled, "Yeah," and another whistled).

She said, 'Hello, country bumpkin.'

How's the frost out on the pumpkin?

I've seen a lot of sights but, man, you're something.

Where'd you come from, country bumpkin?'

(More audience yelling of enthusiasm.)

After Angela finished singing the song, an elderly lady climbed unsteadily on the stage. A younger woman assisted her in walking. The older lady was sobbing, "Child, you made me cry; I cannot help it; between sobs, she said, "My country bumpkin died two months ago, and I miss him."

Angela hugged her, "I'm sorry, grandmother."

"No, don't be sorry; I needed to cry; I have not been able to cry. Thank you." As the lady turned to walk off the stage she said, "Bless you, sweetheart. By Now!" The crowd was very quiet; soft, respectful applause followed the elderly lady as she made her way to her table.

An un-nerved, teary-eyed Angela took a few minutes to dab at her eyes as she walked to the music sound man to regain emotional strength to start the next song, "If we get this kind of reaction to every song, it is going to be a rough night."

She sang more songs, took a fifteen-minute break, and finished the evening. There were no disturbances for the crowd had become amazingly attentive, respectful, and quiet for the Country Music Club. The club owner noticed a change also; bartenders and servers noticed an increase in the amount of drinks ordered. That pleased the owner who commented that maybe we should put her on the payroll full time. Angela and the club crowd were a good "fit." The commitment as it was "sold" to the owner was about 2 hours of singing with at least a fifteen-minute break; but nobody was counting or keeping track of time, the number of songs, or how much time was taken between songs. Many people filed by the "tip jar," a big gold fish bowl on a table near the entrance and dropped dollar bills into it; a few left larger bills. Bruno, the bouncer, kept his eye on the bowl. When she finished singing, he put the tip money in a brown envelope and as he handed it to her, he asked her real name; she laughed and said, "Why don't you just call me 'CC' for Chinese Country?" Bruno smiled, "Then CC it is and until the next time take care."

The next time, Angela appeared at the Country Music Club the crowd was larger than the first time. The word had apparently spread about the singing for the people now appeared to be waiting for the program to start. Angela started out with her signature song:

He walked into the bar (There was immediate clapping.) and parked his lankly frame on a tall barstool . . . She continued to sing the song.

There was loud applause after she finished. She acknowledged the clapping and went to the sound man to discuss the next song. This evening was very much like the other night except that she left the stage and walked among the audience between songs. She would stop and talk randomly at different tables and tell them that if they had a request she would try to sing it. If she did not know it, she told them she would work on it the next few days so she could sing it later. Also, this evening she wore a full-length white dress with sleeves, a high neck, and short slits in the bottom of the dress to let her walk more easily. Of course, the major objective was to spot any of the suspects that might have come to see her out of curiosity. She did see several Chicago Police Department officers with their smiling faces scattered throughout the audience; they identified themselves with a special gesture of their hands as they placed their hands at a special place on their faces. What she did not know was that the police officers had been fussing among themselves as to which ones were going to the show because they all wanted to go. Again, as she finished the program, Bruno had the brown envelope ready for her, "Good night, CC; be careful out there."

"Thank you, Bruno, I will be careful."

The task force was eagerly waiting for any news of an appearance of the suspects. They reasoned it might take a while longer for the news to reach their intended targets simply because it took time for word about something like this to travel around the city. Again, she showed up at the Country Music Club; again she sang her signature song; again she walked throughout the audience to chat with the patrons but this time it was different. She spotted the table with three young looking Chinese males who were pretending to be consumed with their drinks but were actually keeping a close look at her. She wore a black pant suit with a black belt tonight; like her dresses before the pant suit did not exaggerate her figure, but was modest and had good class. As she walked around the tables she was very nervous and could feel their eyes upon her; she deliberately kept her back to their table and avoided any eye contact with them. When she reached a table next to their table, it was too much for them and one of them yelled at her, "Come over here, baby."

She gave him a cold, icy look, "And, why should I come to your table? Do you not know how to greet a lady with something other than "baby?"

"We want to know if you are from China," was his response.

She unloaded on him in Chinese, "It is none of your business where I am from, and if you cannot tell by now I am from China, you may not be playing with a full deck!"

The two companions now started picking on the third one and were speaking Chinese, "Guess she told you, retard; you got shot out of the saddle, you reject," the second one said.

The third one persisted, "You don't (in Chinese) have to be such a smart-ass. I just wanted to make conversation with someone who is also from our country."

Angela now lowered the boom, "I do not care (in Chinese) where you are from but as you are obviously from China I especially do not want to meet anyone other than someone I already know who is from China; I have no desires about having a country-warming home coming; you little boys need to learn some manners about how to approach a lady and to learn how to talk to someone and to use language other than what you might use to pick up a street-walker whom you would "bang-bang" when you got them home."

As Angela continued to greet people at other tables she faintly heard the three suspects commenting (again, in Chinese), "Wow, she is a real, genuine, cold-hearted bitch" one of them said. Another said, "Who does she think she is anyway?" Then their conversation faded away as the noise in the room overwhelmed any talk between them.

What she did not hear was how they decided to find out as much information about her from their contacts in China.

Angela was trembling as she walked around a little more to calm her nerves. If these three were the ones, contact had been made. She realized she now had to reel them in much as you might with a fish that has taken the bait on the fishing hook, easily and "steady as it goes"! There was nothing more to do tonight except to finish the evening's program, take her "brown bag" from Bruno, and report progress of the night. The Chicago police officers, who were poised discreetly to pounce upon these nationals if the need arose, observed she spoke to the three fellows in Chinese; the officers had developed protective feelings toward Angela and admired her courage to attempt such an assignment. Bruno, also, kept his eyes on her as she performed and as she walked throughout the audience; if someone so much as laid an unwelcome hand on her or patted her rear end, he was ready to jump on them like a Grizzly bear. By now, she had developed this little ritual with Bruno, "By now, take care of yourself, CC."

"Yes, I will, Bruno, not to worry."

She was happy for this one night to end. After reporting what had taken place, the prevailing mood of the task force was to do nothing; let the bait sink in, let them think about their encounter with the "ice queen," and wait to see what their response would be. That suited Angela.

SETTING THE HOOK

The next scheduled evening of singing was going as usual when Angela was singing her signature song except that a tsunami of emotions about her childhood suddenly flooded over her that distracted from the singing. She stopped singing to talk to the audience, "I need to tell you a few things about myself before I finish this song. My home is in the country in China. Just as many of you grew up on farms and migrated to this great city, I too have migrated to this great country to make my home. I cannot return to my country; tonight the emotions of homesickness and of missing my family overwhelmed me. Unless you have experienced this a person does not know what it is like to be uprooted from what is so familiar to you. This city has people from the other continents of the world and we have this in common that we left homes to come here. It is said that a person can never return home; home is never the same as what you remembered. I can never fish with my grandfather again in his little pond on his farm; I will never again feel my grandfather rub my legs after I have fallen down and scratched them. Please forgive me for my childlike emotional display." She then finished the song:

And she said, "So long, country bumpkin / The frost is gone now from the pumpkin / I've seen some sights and life's been somethin' / See you later, country bumpkin."

There was hardly a dry eye in the Country Music Club. The hard-cases and tough guys melted when thoughts of home, mother, and childhood filled their minds; the crowd was amazingly quiet for there was a collective reflection on matters of life. There were three young men who did not miss Angela's comment about not being able to go home; these three guys now had the code name "the boys" after she chewed them out at the last night she sang. It was not coincidence that their table was surrounded by tables the Chicago Police officers occupied; the officers blended. When Angela walked through the crowd the special signal indicated who they were; it was all she could do to keep from laughing as she noticed how they sat next to the boys. The officers had named the boys; for example, boy # 1 who assumed leadership of the group; boy # 2 who was more introverted; and boy # 3 who did not seem like he knew what was happening but was along for the ride. When she got close to their table, #1 asked her if she would join their group for they wanted to tell her something. After she sat down, #1 told her they were sorry about how they had treated her last time and said that they had gotten her a gift. She refused to take it, but they insisted.

Then the boys wanted to find out more about her. They asked her if it was true that she had escaped from Chinese authorities because of a trial in Changsha. And, is that also why you cannot go back to China because of the court trial. She told them yes in both cases; it was apparent to Angela they had done some investigation. Then they said that they were not Han Chinese; well, yes, she knew that but they, of course, knew she was Han. And, they asked her how she felt about the current Chinese regime and if she blamed it for her situation. She was very cautious about her comments; she said that she blamed some bad individuals for her situation. They asked if she would like to do something to get back at them.

She responded that she had no idea of what she could do. She thought it was a good time to break off conversation so she said, "Look at the time. I must get back to the stage. Thank you for your gift." Number 1 said that they would have something very exciting to tell her the next time. As she walked back to the stage she believed something was about to happen. When she reported to the task force, the advice was the same: steady as she goes.

Angela thought often of her grandfather but never so strongly as at this moment. She remembered how he took her fishing in his little pond and the rituals they went through; for example, he explained to her how they had to select a proper fishing pole and they looked for a suitable sprout to cut to make her pole; next, he had to get a strong string and hook for her complete with a float or cork; and then the bait such as worms or something equally suitable.

And, they would sit on the pond bank, anchor their poles, and he would say, "Now, we wait. Much of fishing is patience. Watch the float to see if it moves, or if it goes under water then you must be careful to "set the hook" or you might lose the fish." To set the hook he showed her how to jiggle the pole a little to sink the hook into the fish.

"Did I do it right, Grandfather?" she asked.

"You sure did, Lotus Blossom," he told her. "Now, we can eat fish for supper. Get on my back and let's take these fish to grandmother for her to cook." Then he kneeled on one knee so she could climb on his back and put her arms around his neck; he put his arms under her legs and locked his fingers in front of him. Angela remembered these times as some of the happiest in her childhood and in her entire life. Her grandfather was a survivor of the "Long March" and a respected member in the community. She got too big for him to carry her on his back but they still went fishing together as long as he was able.

She remembered his traditional Chinese funeral when he died. The family and friends carried his casket to the burial spot on the side of a hill; the people constantly shot off firecrackers to "wake" the ancestors that he was joining them. Then every year thereafter she remembered her grandfather and grandmother as the family would "sweep the tomb" on tomb sweeping day to clean the burial site from growth of brush and weeds; also, they would use firecrackers to let them know they were there and the family would burn some fake money for them. These were the memories that suddenly flooded over her and caused her emotionalism.

She approached the next singing time intrepidly. She did not want to go but knew she could not back out now. The evening started the same as always but when she took her break "the boys" were insistent she join them to hear the "news." She appeared casually with nonchalance at their table. Number 1 began to rattle away (in Chinese) about their great news.

She seemed mildly interested in what he was going to tell her, "So, what is the big secret?"

He started to explain, "You know we are members of a minority that has a big complaint about the Chinese government; we have planned to do something in the United States to bring that government under suspicion from Americans that the government is sabotaging United States society.

"Really?" Angela said in shock. "And, what might that be?" she asked skeptically.

Now, #1 smiled with self-satisfaction, "We have set explosives in the Willis Tower to detonate at 12:00pm midnight tonight."

"And, just how have you been able to do something like that?" she asked in disbelief.

Now, #2 entered the conversation, "We work in the food service in the tower and have worked there several months. Many times we have carried bags of Russet potatoes into the food service areas past the guards who showed little interest in a sack of potatoes. And, plastic explosives can be molded and shaped by hand to resemble, let's say, potatoes. And, then with some spray paint and a little dirt spread around on them, the molded explosives could pass for real potatoes. Also our work passes give us the run of the building so that we might enter into the stairways and little corridors of places where maintenance workers often go and, more importantly, where the steel posts that support the big tower could be accessed. So, we taped in some of the "potatoes" in places that are little hideaways."

Angela's reaction was to tell them she believed they were full of "blarney" or BS and were blowing hot air. "That is simply a lot of bull," she concluded, "and I have to go to the bathroom before finishing the show." As she headed for the bathroom, nobody paid any attention to another lady who followed her closely into the bathroom.

As quickly as she could when she entered the bathroom, she checked to see if the stalls were empty and they were. It did not matter so much, she believed, because she would speak Chinese and who there would understand her? She had to get the information to the task force as quickly as possible as time was running out so she took a chance, broke protocol, and contacted Chief Investigator Liao, "Chief, it is happening tonight. The boys have set explosives in the Willis Tower and have set the detonators at 12:00pm midnight tonight. They used plastic explosives and molded it to look like potatoes."

"Thank you, message understood," Liao replied, "and, Angela, get out of there as quickly as you can."

"Yes, Chief," with pleasure she said as she dropped her cell phone in a toilet and flushed it. As she exited the stall, she heard this voice say, "You Han bitch," and then she felt this hard blow to the back of her head and she fell to the floor.

The nondescript lady who followed her into the bathroom was also Chinese who had been in the United States for many years and did not attract attention as a foreigner. She was also sweet on #1 of the boys and was getting pretty upset about his interest in Angela. When she heard her brief words to Liao, she went immediately to the boys' table and told them that their newly found friend was a secret Chinese agent who was blowing the whistle on their plans. The boys got up slowly and appeared to be going to the bathroom; the bathrooms were located on the other side of the stage and close to one of the five exits. The bathroom doors were not visible from the entrance to the club, nor from the vantage point of the Chicago Police officers. So, neither Bruno nor the officers saw them enter the ladies' bathroom. They got inside the bathroom just briefly before Angela exited the stall; then they waylaid her. Number 1 hit her in the back of her head; she fell on the floor then the three of them jumped on her and hit her in the face around her eyes and kicked her torso; and #1 especially was full of hate and grabbed her hair and used it to beat her head on the concrete floor.

Bruno thought it was taking too much time for her to get back to finish the evening. He suspiciously moved around the stage to the bathroom and when he heard commotion inside he plunged through the door and when he saw what was happening he lunged toward the three boys; he picked #1 up as if he were a sack of groceries and whirled him around and around to use him as a club to knock the other two boys down and up against the walls; he then threw #1 as hard as possible against yet another wall. He kneeled over Angela, took off his coat, laid it tenderly over her, and yelled out the door for an ambulance. He went back to her prostrate body and sat on his haunches to watch over her; he shook with emotion, adrenalin flow, and regret that he had not prevented this. The bathroom immediately filled with Chicago Police officers who took "the boys" out of the room and set guard to the entrance.

The EMT crew showed up immediately as they came from the Chicago Medical Center that was not far from the club. They praised Bruno for not touching or moving her and covering her with his coat; they prepared her for the trip to the Trauma Center, loaded her gently into the ambulance, and with Bruno made their way the few blocks to the center where the full staff of doctors and nurses were ready to take care of her. The staff stopped Bruno from going inside but told him they would keep him up-dated on her condition.

The EMT people told Bruno that it looked very bad for she obviously had brain trauma. Those kind of injuries are very unpredictable according to them.

Bruno planted himself there for the long haul. After at least 45 minutes to one hour, the chief trauma doctor, Dr. Schmitt, came out to tell Bruno they had stabilized her and were taking her to a room in the intensive care unit. She also told him no visitors would be allowed except family; she gave him her personal direct phone number so he could check on her. Bruno thanked her very much. Before he left he found the EMTs who took her to the center; after he explained who he was and why he was interested, he asked them if they would or could tell him her condition when they delivered her to the center. Very quietly they said she would have died had it not been for Dr. Schmitt who would not give up on her.

THE PRIDE OF CHICAGO

When Liao received Angela's message, he immediately contacted Matthews. Matthews contacted the Chicago Police Department and the police responded with their bomb squads and descended upon the Willis Tower. They barricaded streets; the fire department also arrived with ladder trucks. They began to review pictures from the surveillance cameras.

Fortunately, the building was occupied only by maintenance people at this late hour. The Chicago PD asked them to leave the building but most of them refused, "This is our building; we know more about it than anybody else; we know the little nooks and crannies better than your bomb squads; nobody is going to blow our building if we can stop it. Let us help."

One of the seasoned maintenance personnel began to talk about "The Pride of Chicago" in terms only engineers might understand. If these guys think a small amount of explosives can bring down the Willis Tower, they do not know anything about its construction. This building used a new construction process called "bundled tube structure" that is much stronger than traditional steel girders; the bundled tubes are connected and gives the building more strength. The tubes have more resistance to strong winds and have more rigidity. They are welded together and support each other; the strong winds from across the Illinois prairies cause the building to gently sway as it is designed to do. However, he concluded, that is no reason not to take an explosive charge seriously.

Another person suggested that this attempt was out-of-date, that is, bomb attacks now target populations, not property. Property can be rebuilt; people are gone. For example, contrast the Boston Marathon bomb with the garage bomb at the World Trade Center in New York City; the garage bomb did little damage but the Boston bomb killed and injured several people. These guys are amateurs.

The police frantically scanned the recordings of the surveillance cameras. They looked at the day closest to the time of detonation— 12:00pm midnight. Also, they scanned the first three floors because they reasoned the bombers would want to set explosives at the bottom of the building.

The police were correct. The pictures showed three fellows walking into a remote part of the first floor. One of them carried a sack on his shoulder; the other two followed.

They disappeared through a door leading to a stairway to the very bottom of the building. The bomb squads immediately started searching that part of the building. Several maintenance workers also followed and began to look for little cubbyhole places that would conceal a bomb.

Time was now the enemy. It was after 11:00pm. That did not deter these workers. Finally, they saw a brown bulky looking bulge wedged between some water pipes and the round "structured tubes" of the foundation. The bomb experts ordered everyone out of the way as they approached the bomb. It looked as if it had been dropped in between the water pipes and the tubes. As they looked at it, one of them said, "We don't have much time to 'admire' this thing; we need to get it out."

The maintenance crew produced some stiff wire coat hangers. The bomb squad quickly saw their idea. They straightened the wire, then curved it, and pushed it under the bottom of the sack. Then they pushed more wire under and around the sack to form a cradle; very carefully they pulled the sack out of its resting place until they could reach it with their hands. Now, they could gently slide the bomb along the water pipes until they could physically lower it to the floor. When they cut away the sack they could see the exposed explosives and the detonator.

One look at the detonator was all they needed. They popped the top off the timer and clipped the wire that was attached to the clock. The time was 11:55pm.

ANGELA'S FANTASIES

The lights went out with Angela as everything turned black. She had sensations of being on the cold concrete floor; she wondered why she was there. This big hulk of a man was sitting on the floor and watching over her. That must be Bruno; why was he here and not at the entrance to the club? The next feeling she had was the motion of the stretcher as the EMTs wheeled her into a waiting vehicle that roared off with lights flashing and a siren blowing.

When the vehicle stopped the same fellows whisked her out of the vehicle into a large room where many people with white and blue frocks surrounded and began to examine her. And, those lights were so bright! The lights would go out and darkness would take over but the lights came back. After what seemed like an eternity the rolling of a stretcher gave her a feeling of motion; finally, the stretcher stopped, a few women dressed in white fussed around the room and hooked several tubes to her and wrapped heated warm blankets around her. The warmness was very comforting; she wanted to sleep; the darkness returned.

Suddenly, bright lights appeared again to push the darkness away. A lady in white was looking into her eyes with a light that blinded her; take that light away was her immediate reaction. The lady persisted, pushed her eyelids open, and looked into both eyes. Enough, enough, Angela screamed but she did not make a sound; it was only in her mind. The darkness finally returned; she felt as though she was floating and drifting around in the bed as though she were intoxicated; the bed seemed to rock and to roll around.

Then she heard a voice calling to her, "Let's go, Lotus Blossom, or the fish will get tired of waiting for us and will go to the bottom of the pond."

"Grandfather, what are you doing here?" she asked.

"I am waiting for you so we can go fishing," he replied.

Jack appeared at the side of the bed, grabbed her hand, and started asking questions, "Where are you, Angela, what are you doing in bed?"

She answered, "I am right here; why do you keep asking me those questions?" Of course, there was nothing to hear from her; she remained silent.

Jack continued to ask more questions and threatened to do things to her like tickle her feet if she did not answer him. She answered in her mind, "Jack, you are beginning to get on my nerves. You keep asking the same questions over and over; you should know the answers by now as many times as I have told you!"

Then the lady in white, probably a doctor Angela concluded, again shined the light into her eyes. It was bright and pushed away the darkness; then the doctor left; Angela cried out to her to stay for she did not like the darkness, but the doctor did not hear anything.

"What is happening to me?" Angela wondered to herself. The lady in white comes in and tortures me with bright lights; Jack is driving me crazy with his questions over and over; and my grandfather is waiting for me to go fishing. She decided the easy thing to do was to simply go with her grandfather to the little pond and fish; fishing would be a relief, a comfort, and it would be quiet in her childhood home. She would also see her grandmother. But, she did not think that would be right for she had a job, and she could not run off and away from her duties. She did not like the darkness; she did not want to stay in the darkness. Time passed; how much time? She had no idea of time.

"Oh, no," she thought as the lady in white appeared again. Again, the bright lights pushed the darkness aside, "Please stay," Angela yelled at her but she turned and went out the door. Next, she had to put up with Jack asking questions.

Suddenly, she felt somebody rubbing her legs. "Grandfather?" she asked. "No, it is not me rubbing your legs, I am waiting for you to go fishing, remember?" her grandfather replied.

She could not stand the mystery of who was rubbing her legs and she tried and tried until she opened her eyes to see Jack washing her feet and rubbing her legs, "Jack, what the hell are you doing?"

This time Jack heard her and replied automatically, "I am washing your stinky feet."

At the moment, she said something; the doctor came in to look at her and Angela asked, "Will you grab my hand and hold on to it? Squeeze it hard; it feels so good!"

The doctor asked, "How are you feeling?"

"I guess I am all right. I don't know how I am," was her reply. When the doctor started to leave, Angela cried out, "Please don't leave me. I don't want to go back (to the darkness); I want to stay out here; I want to live; I want to be in the light; hold on to my hand; don't let them pull me back; I want to walk; I want to see trees; it is not time for me to join them!"

The doctor squeezed her hand and said, "We are not letting you go anywhere. Who is trying to pull you back?"

Angela answered, "My grandfather. He wants to take me fishing. And, my grandmother who is waiting at the house. I don't want to go with them right now. I am too young to join them!"

The doctor replied, "We will keep you out."

The doctor held on to her hand tightly but sent orders to a nurse to prepare an injection of some sort and to bring it to her. When the nurse came with the shot, the doctor told Jack to clear out because they needed to do some things and she told Angela, "Young lady, we are getting you ready for a little walk. Do you think you will like that?"

"Yes, yes," Angela replied with tears in her eyes.

After about 20 minutes, the doctor summoned Jack and told him to help Angela take her first walk down the hall; she had a walker to steady herself and a belt around her waist for Jack to hold on to as a safety precaution.

WHAT IS HAPPENING?

Holding on to Liao's hand, Jack gazed around the room and feebly asked, "What is happening?"

Matthews, who had his hand on Jack's back said quietly and close to his ear, "There are many things you need to know but now is not the time. Soon everything will be explained but now Dr. Schmitt, the trauma doctor, will tell you what to expect when you walk through this other door!" Matthews stepped aside as the physician approached Jack and laid her hand on his shoulder and looked at him. Liao likewise moved aside and somewhat behind Jack.

Dr. Schmitt called for two chairs as she began to tell Jack what to expect, and she placed one hand on his knee. "Jack," she began, "what you will see beyond that door will shock you! You see, Angela is in the next room, and she is in a coma. She is fighting for her life!"

Jack reacted predictably. He stared at Dr. Schmitt for a few minutes and then with an emotional voice asked brokenly, "Angela? In a coma?"

"Yes," she said, "and Jack, straighten up and get strong because there is no time for your emotionalism because she needs you."

Jack asked, "How did this happen?"

Both Matthews and Liao comforted him but said there is no time. Liao added that Angela needed him as she had never needed anyone.

Dr. Schmitt took over and described Angela's situation, "A person in a coma tends to turn off the switch to reality in their mind. The shock of the trauma to the brain causes it to withdraw as a defensive mechanism to the injury. It is as if the person is hiding from reality somewhere inside their brain. We never know how long a coma may last; they are unpredictable; some last minutes, hours, and some last for years. Some last until death! We believe the sooner we try to 'make contact' or to 'find' the person hiding inside their brain the better; we believe the patient usually decides to come back themselves; there is no way of making them return. Jack, look at me and listen carefully, you are to go in there, act strongly, forcefully, and to find Angela! Do you understand?"

"What will I ask?" he asked.

"You are her love, you know her, you know her weaknesses, you know how to 'turn her on'! That is what you must do: turn her on because she is turned off!"

"But it might be embarrassing!"

"Don't be silly," Dr. Schmitt said, "I am a doctor; there is nothing you might do or say I have not heard or seen. A life is at stake; are you ready to go in there, to hold her hand, and to go to work on her?"

"Yes," responded an energized Jack.

Then she and Jack walked into the room where Angela laid on a bed with several tubes running to her. Jack staggered and faltered but Dr. Schmitt said, "No, no, Jack, grab her hand and get to it!"

Jack then sat in a chair, took her hand, turned, and looked at the doctor who gave him an impatient gesture toward Angela, and asked, "Angela, what are you doing in bed and what have you been doing to be in bed?" The doctor gave him a gesture to keep it going.

While you are in bed I had to fix my breakfast this morning! What do you mean to be up here in bed? I think I will give you a good spanking for "gold bricking" like this. Jack glanced at the doctor who voiced with her lips, "more, more"! Where are you anyway? Why don't you talk to me? Another thing I am thinking about is to put some duct tape around your ankles and to tickle your feet. What about that? How would you like that? And, while I am at it, I might as well pinch one or two of your titties; Jack looked at the doctor who gave him the okay sign as she stifled a little giggle.

Dr. Schmitt turned to leave and told Jack there would be a bed rolled in for him to stay there and to keep this up over and over.

Jack continued to talk to Angela. He went over the same things and added a few more. The doctors came in to check her condition. Her automatic biological functions worked but she just was away somewhere. At the end of the day, Jack fell into the bed exhausted and wondered what the morning would bring; he slept soundly.

The next morning started with more of the same. Dr. Schmitt encouraged Jack to keep it up. He did and then unexpectedly another person entered the room with the doctor, a very large man named "Bruno."

"Bruno is the man who saved Angela," the doctor said.

Bruno said, "No, no, you saved her after the other docs gave up on her; but you saw a small movement in her chest."

"Okay, go see her and talk to her, Bruno!"

He held her hand, stood there like a tree, and blubbered like a baby as he said between sobs, "I am your 'Country Bumpkin', CC; I have come to see you. Wake up, CC!"

When Bruno left Jack asked what in the world was that about? The answer was the same as what he was told in the beginning, all in good time!

Another day and night passed. Angela's condition stabilized; she breathed on her own; the doctors removed the tubes except for the feeding tube.

Jack asked Dr. Schmitt if he might wash her feet and tickle them. "Sure," she replied.

He got a pan of warm to hot water, pulled her feet up and put them in the water and began to wash her feet and ankles. Suddenly, he heard this weak voice say, "Jack, what the hell are you doing?"

Without even thinking he answered, "I am washing your stinky feet!"

It feels so good why don't you wash the rest of me?

"Give me time and don't start fussing; I just started on your feet!" Jack answered.

"Oh, oh, I hurt when I move," Angela said, "what happened to me?"

Jack asked, "What do you remember? Do you know where you were?"

"All I remember is going to the bathroom and then waking up because somebody, probably you, has been tickling my feet, and then you are washing my feet. Also, I dreamed Bruno came to see me. Nothing else is there," Angela replied.

At that time, Dr. Schmitt walked into the room and said to Angela, "I am Dr. Schmitt and I have been taking care of you. How do you feel?"

"I guess I am all right. I don't know how I am." The doctor looked at Jack, smiled, and nodded her head for him to leave. She looked at Angela and said, "I am one of the people who is going to make you whole! Do you know your name? Do you know where you are? Do you know how long you have been here?"

"My name is Angela, but I do not know where I am nor how long I have been here and I do not know what happened to me."

While Dr. Schmitt was checking her over Dr. Reidaman came into the room and began to look into her eyes with a light, and asked her to move her eyes to follow the light, and talked gently to her, "You have given us a real scare, young lady, you have some bruises around your eyes and some large lumps in the back of your head, but unlike Humpty Dumpty, we are going to put you back together; that is what we do here!" The doctors worked together checking her over—does this hurt? How does this feel? Take a deep breath—the doctors were pleased with the responses.

We are going to leave you briefly, but there is someone who has waited a long time to see you. And, they motioned for this person to come into the room as they waved goodbye.

"Hello, Angela. How are you?" Chief Investigator Liao asked as he slowly walked up to her, bent over her, and kissed her gently on her cheek.

"I am sore all over, Chief; did we get them?" was her immediate response.

"Yes, we got all three of them!"

"Oh, no," Angela grimaced as she attempted to raise up a little to say, "there were four of them—three guys and a woman!"

Liao looked stunned and thought for a moment, "We found the explosives and neutralized the triggering devices. You saved the tower from a bomb."

"No, you guys saved the tower; I just gave you the information."

"You need to rest," Liao said, "and I am alerting the others about the woman. Do you know who saved you? You know how Bruno always watches you?"

"Yes, I know," she said.

When you went to the bathroom he thought you were taking longer than usual and he headed to the bathroom and went inside. He saw the three guys beating you; one was banging your head on the floor. In a rage he picked up the one slamming your head and whirled him around to knock the other two against the wall, and then he threw him against the wall. All three slumped on the floor unconscious. He then yelled outside to get an ambulance, took off his coat, and covered you. Of course, his big coat was like a blanket. He kneeled, looked over you; but he knew not to touch or move you. That is how the EMT people found you. Bruno saved you.

And when you got to the University of Chicago trauma center, the team began working on you. After about 15 minutes, the doctors except for Dr. Schmitt had given up on you. She saw slight movement in your chest and would not give up; she got you working again.

Angela got emotional as she realized how close to death she had been and how her guardian friend Bruno had stopped the beating. Her emotionalism was interrupted when Dr. Shmott came into the room with a couple of nurses and said, "Time for girl stuff; we need privacy."

Liao kissed Angela on the hand and said, "I am in the next room."

TIME FOR THE CHICKENS TO ROOST

"The next room" was operational headquarters for the team of home security, Illinois State Police, the Chicago Police Department, and the Chinese investigators. And, there was Jack.

Jack was increasingly frustrated and fed up about not knowing anything about anything. He confronted Liao, "We have an expression: 'It is time for the chickens to roost'! It is time for the chickens to roost; it is time to tell me what is happening!"

"All right, I agree," Liao replied. Let's start, as one of your other expressions says, at the beginning." Jack nodded his head and kept looking at him.

Liao continued, "We have dissident groups in China, some who are insurgents who would like to overthrow our government. We keep surveillance on them. Some of them leave China; some come to the United States; these few came to Chicago."

"So," said a skeptical Jack.

"So," is that we need to know what these people are doing. Their level of hatred is very strong, and they would do anything to cause a conflict between our countries, and, at the least, cause embarrassment of our government."

Again, the skeptical, "So."

We contacted our counterparts in your government and explained how we would assist in any way possible to prevent and/ or to apprehend these nationals who are capable of inflicting great damage.

"Angela," said Liao softly, "is one of our most skillful operatives."

This information stunned Jack; he took a few moments to focus and to regain his composure to ask, "You must be kidding."

Very seriously Liao said, "I never kid about my work and national security!" Chan even now had a serious face.

"But, how in the world . . . ?" Jack asked, "Do I fit into all this?"

"You were not supposed to happen," Liao added.

"We sent Angela to Changsha College to sharpen her American English language skills so she could pass in the United States as a more or less disgruntled Chinese national who could identify with these dissident groups. And, then she met you."

You make it sound like she met some sort of pariah.

"No, not at all. What about the incident at her school, the trial, the boat trip on the Yangtze, and the ocean-going freighter?"

"All part of the big plan," Liao answered

"My role then in this 'big plan' was basically that of a patsy," Jack said disgustingly.

"No, no, no, you are looking at the glass being half empty; look at the glass as being half full; after she met you and knew of our plan to plant her in Chicago, she would not budge without you. She threatened to quit and to teach. You became the key to the whole plan," Liao affirmed.

"Oh, really?" Jack said with sarcasm.

"Yes. It is hard to imagine the suspicions these groups have of other Chinese; Angela's story had to be convincing and fool proof. We did not know how to get her into Chicago without creating suspicion. You became the answer. She had to be in a situation where the dissidents would approach her, not for her to approach them. She had to be genuine, Jack, or the whole thing would have gone down the drain. She convinced and fooled Wolfman," smiled Liao.

Jack's astonishment surfaced, "You know about Wolfman?"

"Oh, hell, Jack, we have known about Wolfman for years. He is harmless. And, Hogjowl is also well known to us." At this comment Chan beamed with his famous smile, and Jack was compelled to laugh.

Again, Jack asked where he and Angela fit into the big picture.

"Okay," said Liao, "you do not know what Angela did! As these nationals saw her, they investigated and heard she had left China to avoid a sentence for anti-government activity and foreign-influence peddling, she skipped out on her trial, and authorities tried to find her but she gave them the slip. This convinced them to contact her and to see if she had ill-will toward our government; after all, she had lost her teaching job and was a fugitive from justice. And that she is pretty did not hurt the situation either.

"But, how did she end up in this hospital?" asked an impatient Jack.

"There is more to the story", Liao continued, "these characters took her into their confidence and told her they planned to blow up the Willis Tower, formerly Sears Tower. She made a careless mistake when she called us with the information for she knew she had to get the information to us quickly before the explosives would self-detonate. Someone heard her call us and tipped them off; consequently, they beat her up. But, Jack, she thwarted the plot to blow up the Willis Tower!"

Jack looked incredulously at Liao to say, "You are telling me this planning and effort was to save the tower and Angela actually saved the tower?"

Liao countered, "We did not know what they were up to, if anything at all, but we did not want to take any chances. And, yes, all this effort was to stop them from doing something, whatever it was. When they heard that Angela was talking to authorities, they retaliated and attempted to kill her in their angry revenge; this is when Bruno enters the story. He saved her from the three men.

A still puzzled Jack asked, "Who is Bruno and how did these dissidents know her in order to contact her?"

Liao looked pleased with himself when he answered, "That is how the cultural programs and bi-lingual language programs help. You know she has a powerful and beautiful voice. The Illinois authorities, city and state police, leaned on a club owner to add her to their night club entertainment. This club is in a part of town where country music people live, people who have migrated to Chicago, and near where we thought the nationals lived. The club billed her on the flashing marquee as 'Chinese Country Bumpkin!' The song, 'Hello Country Bumpkin' was her featured song; she opened with that song. Word spread and soon the curious nationals came to hear and to see her and discovered she was the real thing. They contacted her. Bruno is the bouncer because this place attracts tough people, but when Angela opened up and belted out the country bumpkin song, most of these tough guys and women turned to mush; many teared up because this song reminded them of their roots on farms and their country homes. It was too much for them. They love Angela and call her their country bumpkin or some call her 'CC' for Chinese country bumpkin. And, especially big, bad, bouncer Bruno would tear up every time she sang that song."

"How did this happen and I am now just finding out about it?" Jack asked.

Liao explained, "We believed it was better that you did not know. Angela left every Friday to be with her friends on her 'girls' night out' and would drive to that big barn down the road. She parked the car inside, and we helicoptered her to the copter pad at the University of Chicago Medical Center; in about 10 minutes after riding in a limousine she entered the club as the 'Chinese Country Bumpkin.'"

An amazed Jack said, "That explains why she kept singing and practicing these old country songs like Tom T. Hall's song about kids, old dogs and watermelon wine. That one makes me cry just to think about it."

Jack continued, "Why have we not heard about this in the news?" Liao answered, "The news stations did cover and report the event as they reported an anonymous tip led to the apprehension and arrest of three Chinese nationals who were plotting to bomb the tower. Technically, it was a tip. There was no need to tell who it was for if her name were revealed, her value as an undercover investigator would be over. As it stands people who come to the club think three hoodlums beat her to rob her; they do not need to know she saved the tower."

"What about those contacts with police—in Los Angeles, in Utah, and the national park?" asked Jack.

"That was our way of keeping track of the progress you were making across the country. And, just to check on your safety," Liao replied.

Jack looked nonplused. He felt foolish after finding out the police had them in their sights all along, "What about the trial in Changsha, and the checks on the Yangtze boat ride?" he persisted.

Liao explained, "There was an incident at the school but we exaggerated it to cause a trial. The judge was never aware of the greater plan but events fell into place. And, the headmaster of the school was real and genuine, the ass that he is; all of this had to be real enough to believe and to convince you to "rescue" Angela. The checks on Hogjowl were to keep him honest, that is, to keep him from robbing you or doing worse things. You were at risk with Hogjowl; he is capable of serious mischief; but Chan made a believer out of him or as you say here "stopped him from sucking eggs.""

"This knocks the wind out of my sail," said Jack, "it makes me feel like a real stooge, like a state prop."

"We have had this conversation before," Liao continued, "it would not have worked without you; you were an essential part of the plan. Even Chan did not know about Angela."

"But you pretended not to know her," Jack said.

"You had to be convinced, or you would have had suspicions," countered Liao.

An exhausted Liao and Jack became quiet and looked thoughtful. Neither said anything for some time as they reflected on these events.

Finally, Jack stood up, walked around a little, and said, "When the chickens came home to roost, they really roosted, didn't they? It's time for me to check on Angela." He headed toward the door to her room, but before he entered, he asked Liao one more thing. "What about me and Angela?"

Liao emphasized, "What is between you and Angela is between you and Angela."

THE WALK

With Dr. Schmitt's help Angela slowly and cautiously eased off the bed and put both feet on the floor, "My feet tingle, she said. "Your nerves are waking up," the doctor explained, "they will stop tingling after you walk. It is the other nerves around your body that concerns me. We will know more about the extent of injury when that happens. And, don't set any track record walking down the hall! Take one step at a time; you are a long way from being out of the woods."

After walking about ten steps, Angela commented, "She is right. My body hurts all over, and these feet are tingling like hundreds of little needles are sticking in them. Let's pause for a minute so I can get my breadth."

"Okay," said Jack, "and maybe you can tell me more about what has been happening?" "Let's not spoil a beautiful moment. When it is time I will tell you the whole big story. Right now, let me walk, let me enjoy the light, let me feel life." "Of course. It is too soon. You are right. It is probably time to return to the room."

Neither of them noticed a house keeper who was making her daily rounds of cleaning.

They returned to the room and Dr. Schmitt smiled and laughed, "How are you doing?" she asked. Angela's reply was that her body did not want to work; the doctor replied that that was normal and not to expect too much too fast. And, if your body does not limber up soon, we may have to call in the Physical Therapists, and, believe me, you do not want the PTs to get into the picture because they do not take NO for an answer. She added, "You have walked on your own today because you want to; maybe we can skip PT if you progress daily."

As the doctor turned to leave, Angela panicked and asked her to stay. "Do not worry, I will check on you, but you will have less and less need of me; that is what happens; my patients get well and go their own way."

Angela almost cried, "But, you pulled me out of the darkness. I will always need you!"

"No, no, Angela, you will soon be on your own; your life will resume; you will fight off the darkness yourself. I will be back soon to check on you." And, they hugged.

The walk was the turning point for Angela's recovery. A short amount of exercise did wonders for her confidence; she realized the wisdom of the doctor's comments. The very realistic images of her grandfather began to fade as she began to think of the future. She also realized the job was not complete until this mysterious fourth person was found. She had briefly mentioned she believed there was a woman who had helped "the boys" as she remembered she had heard a woman enter the bathroom immediately after her. The woman had to understand Chinese for she is the one who had to have told the boys about her phone call. When she told Liao of her suspicions, he commented that she was a "needle in the haystack"; however, he showed concern because this woman might want to finish what the boys had tried, that is, to kill Angela. Now, Liao reasoned, she had a personal motive to kill her for as a result of Angela's tip about the plans, the boys were going to be away a long time which would mean #1 was gone from her life.

Liao and Matthews agreed to have a police officer at the door to Angela's room around the clock. This was routine but the complication was there was no suspect and no description of the suspect. It was safe to assume she was Chinese, but police could not interview every Chinese female in Chicago. They believed the best plan was to have a two-pronged approach: 1) provide constant protection for Angela, and 2) to alert police to be looking for a Chinese female that might appear suspicious.

And, since Jack was still staying in the room with her until she was discharged, Liao's mind was temporarily at peace but not completely because he also believed, as Angela, that this was a loose end.

THE WILD CARD

Anybody who has been in the military knows when there is a plan there is a problem. It goes without saying that something is going to happen. Other plans are subject to the same rule of thumb; there is no perfect, foolproof plan. In this case the wild card was the mysterious woman who just happened to understand Chinese; everything would have worked had it not been for this "clinker" or "hair in the butter." It is what it is.

Life in the intensive care unit continued. Angela took a second brief walk and laughed about her "funny feeling" feet and her aches and pains, "They let me know I am living."

The doctor looked into her eyes again, gave a good report, and left her for the day, "You need as much rest as possible so you can face tomorrow with a new lease on life."

After the evening meal and a little bit of television, Angela and Jack decided it was time for her to get some much needed sleep. The day had been exhausting. The nurse made her rounds and checks. Jack tucked Angela in with a warm, heated blanket and decided to take a turn around the care unit before going to bed. On his way back, he chatted briefly with the officer on duty, "Do you need anything?" "No, I am here all night; I will get some coffee later to stay alert. Thanks."

Jack noted Angela was sleeping soundly. He made his little cocoon on the cot; he missed his own bed. All lights were off except for the "don't stumble in the dark lights" or little nightlights located low in the wall to light the floor.

Most people are creatures of habit. Jack was no exception; he went to bed about the same time and woke up about the same time every day. His bladder holding capacity normally lasted until about 3:00am but that was influenced by how much liquid he consumed, if caffeine drinks were involved, and the time he went to bed. For example, if he went to bed late, he would sleep through the night.

This evening was normal. Around 3:00am he responded to the call of nature; he moved silently to the bathroom, left the door slightly ajar so as to not need a light, and did not flush to avoid noise. As he started out of the bathroom he heard commotion outside; he stood in the dark and looked through the partially open door to see what was happening. What he saw caused his hair to stand on end; a small person had entered the room and was making their way toward Angela's bed. When Jack saw a reflection of light off something shiny in the hands of this ghost-like silhouette, he lounged forward to jump on the back of this figure, locked his legs around its torso, and grabbed its right arm with his right hand. The person and Jack fell on the floor and as this mysterious individual struggled they rolled around on the floor; this person had a scalpel in their hand and attempted to slash Jack in many ways; Jack's grip was strong enough to deflect the jabs to small cuts and scratches. He felt like he was riding the back of a Tiger; he knew he could not release his leg lock or his grip on this person's arm. What began as a normal evening became anything but normal.

The noise finally awakened Angela. When she saw the rolling around on the floor, she let out blood-curdling screams that had to wake half of the patients on the floor and got the attention of the nurses who came running. They stepped over the prone police officer and subdued the person that Jack was riding in his jockey shorts and undershirt. Blood was all over the place from the cuts and scratches this individual inflicted on Jack's body. Security showed up and put this slasher who had created this mayhem under control.

Her origin was no secret as she let loose a torrent of "not very nice" Chinese toward Angela who had a look of shock. After police took this woman away, Angela was shaken, and Jack looked like he was bleeding to death from the superficial wounds. The nurses began to clean and to patch the cuts and scratches and were tittering about his shorts and undershirt; Jack made a droll comment, "Have you not seen a guy in shorts before?" "Yes, but not one who has been wrestling with an angry woman armed with a scalpel." And, they giggled even more.

Finally, they got the areas covered with gauze and tape and Jack laid down on his cot with a sarcastic remark, "Now, who is the patient?"

With so much excitement sleep normally would have been out of the question. But, after adrenalin flow often there sets in an exhausted feeling; this happened now as both Angela and Jack had had the scare of their lives. It did not take long before both of them slipped into a deep sleep.

THE WRAP UP

After the night's sleep, Jack awoke in a grumpy mood, "I am getting tired of all this. I want to go home to my plantation, plant some seeds, sit on the front porch, and watch them grow.

Liao who was in the room said, "We have had this conversation before. Look what has happened. We, the team, found the culprits, foiled their plans, and saved no telling how much property destruction and how many lives. And, at no loss of life; there were a couple of close calls to be sure but we got through that also. Was that not worth the effort? Look at the big picture and see the glass half full, not half empty! And, now, it is over; all of this is behind you. You only have to look at the future, and ask yourself, what would have happened if this had not been done? And, how would you feel if you had known you could have done something to stop this and you did nothing? The future looks bright; you and Angela will have to testify at trial; it may be hard to prove the woman, the fourth person, was part of the conspiracy but it should not be difficult to prove an attempted murder charge against her or two attempted murder charges, for that matter. So, Jack, have more patience, sit back, and enjoy the congratulatory comments that will come your way."

An unenthusiastic Jack said, "You are right. I am just tired. And, what happened to the police officer at the door? How did this demon get past him?"

Liao explained how she had gotten a bottle of ether, poured some on a small hand towel, and poured the rest of the bottle over his head as she held the towel over his nose and mouth. She anesthetized him and rendered him unconscious and with the ether on his shirt he was out for some time. It was apparent this person had worked around a hospital as she knew where scalpels were located, where to get the ether, and how to move about the hospital and not attract much attention.

Matthews joined the cozy little group with the comment, "We knew you were a real desperado, Jack, when we picked you up at the farm, but we did not know you were a 'bull rider'."

Jack's mood had improved, "Oh, yes, you learn to do many things when you grow up on the farm. We would ride horses, but one fun activity was to hop on the back of a hog and ride it. Of course, they did not like that and would head for the hog house and scrape us off as they went inside. But I would rather ride a hog any day than that wild woman with a knife in her hand. It has been a long time since I have experienced 'saddle soreness'. We rode the horses 'bare back' as we would just jump on them anywhere and not have to put a saddle and bridle on them. They were used to that and maybe preferred that to a saddle."

Matthews reported the good news. The three suspects were charged, arraigned, and were heading to trial. They looked a little battered as Bruno did a good job of banging them around in the bathroom. The prosecutor does not see any problem with getting a conviction; the defense will be in the public defender's office as they are entitled to a defense. It will be some lame attempt to defend their actions but will not carry much weight. The worst-case scenario is to have to charge them with lesser crimes such as assault and battery, attempted murder, etc. We could think up a few other charges if necessary to keep them around for a long time. And, we have the blessing of the Chinese government that does not want them back or to have to bother with them; their view is to "throw the book at them." Of course, the Chinese want Chief Investigator Liao and

Assistant Investigator Chan to return to China, and he laughed, "Where is Chan, by the way?" Liao smiled, "Oh, his smile got him into some trouble with one of the nurses in the hospital; he is eating breakfast with her."

"I see," continued Matthews, "tell Angela she can return to China anytime she wants, that the judge in Changsha is so happy that she is all right, and that now he wishes he had kissed her on her cheek when she was in his chambers for she is something of a national celebrity for what she has done to help catch these three culprits. But the judge is not too sure of Jack, as he thinks Jack may believe that he 'put one over on him'." Matthews hastened to add, "The judge is simply overjoyed, knows the whole story, and wants to meet Jack whenever it can work out. Also, Angela's status in the United States is not in question; her passport situation will be remedied; she will have to testify at trial. There will be a ceremony after trial to make recognitions, honors, and awards. She might even want to keep 'her job' at the Country Music Club."

THE CEREMONY

The congratulatory ceremony recognized all members of the task force who stopped the plans of the nationalistic terrorists. The Chicago Mayor opened the ceremony as he read a statement from the former Secretary of Homeland Security:

> *Please excuse my absence from today's ceremony for my resignation precludes me from attending such meetings as the secretary. However, I can state my opinions with the proviso that they are my opinions as a citizen of the United States.*
>
> *Terrorists use violence to intimidate people through fear to achieve their objectives that they cannot achieve with peaceful means. Bombings, assassinations, hijackings, kidnappings, and hostage taking are examples of terrorist acts. Minority groups that want to change their governments use terrorism to scare people into accepting their viewpoints.*
>
> *The United States has experienced several acts of violence such as the bomb in the basement of the World Trade Center in 1993, the bombing of the Federal Building in Oklahoma in 1995, and the bomb in the Atlantic Olympic Centennial Park in 1996. Then we enjoyed a few years without such incidents until the 9/11/2001 bombing of the World Trade Center. After that attack we discovered several missed opportunities to do something that would have helped stop it. Former Secretary of State James Baker said, "We just did not connect the dots."*

Since the 9/11 attack many changes have taken place: agencies cooperate more than ever; governments cooperate and share information; there is agreement we are on the same team.

Congratulations to the Chinese government, the Illinois State Police, the Chicago Police Department, and various individuals in Homeland Security. The prevention of the attack on Chicago's Willis Tower is a textbook example of how vigilance and cooperation succeed. Had we ignored the suspicions of the Chinese, had we not formed the task force, had we not worked together, we would not be celebrating in the Willis Tower today. Fighting terrorism is a team effort, not any one part more important than the other, rather all are equally important. That is the way it must be in the future.

The Chicago Mayor now addressed the group:

It is difficult to express how proud I am of the members of this task force who prevented this attack. Members of the Chicago Police Department, I salute you; the Illinois State Police, I commend you; the Chinese investigatory group, I thank you; other individuals who helped, I extend to you our sincere appreciation. For those who are not citizens of the United States, I give you honorary citizenship in the city of Chicago and a Key to the City; know that you are welcome to come to Chicago anytime for the city would not be what it is had it not been for you. The battle is about all of us coming together to stand for what we believe and to protect what we value; we are the community of Chicago and of the world; these acts of violence against property and against lives cannot stand. We must fight them and together we will win as you have shown the world your success.

I now unveil the plaque that recognizes the people who saved this tower from the bomb and the lives that would have been lost. We will put this plaque in the lobby for all

*to see how Chicago shows its pride and its unity in the face
of adversity.*

*Thank you for coming. This concludes our official
ceremony. Please stay, meet and visit with one another. Enjoy
our unlimited and free refreshments.*

Applause ended the talking part of the ceremony. People began
to gather around the plaque to see where their name might be. The
members of the Chicago Police Department who were on the task
force saw their names grouped alphabetically; the Illinois State
Police also had their names grouped similarly; the Chinese names
included Chief Investigator Liao, Assistant Investigator Chan, and
Angela Chou. There were other names such as Bruno Sabetti and
Jack Thomas. Everybody admired the thoughtfulness and beauty of
the plaque.

The party began in earnest. What started as a solemn occasion
now became louder and more raucous for it was a time to celebrate.
Bruno commandeered a table and sat with his legs out from under
the table as they did not fit comfortably; Angela perched on one of
his legs so they would be at eye level with each other, "You know I
can never repay you for saving my life, Bruno," she said.

Bruno would have no part of it, "It is my fault that I did not
prevent them from attacking you. I should have followed them when
they left the table. The doctor saved you!"

"Let me put it another way, then, I do not want to hear any
more guilt talk from you; if it had not been for you I would not be
here. There were others there who did not see the threat also. Will
that make it easier for you?" Angela concluded as she leaned over and
kissed Bruno on his cheek.

"CC, let's enjoy that you are here. Let's put it behind us and
look forward to happy times, let's not have any more talk about it,
okay?" Bruno said with a big smile.

Soon, Jack, Liao, and Matthews gathered around the table as
well. The police officers on the task force stopped to chat. Most of

them asked Angela if she was going to sing again at the Country Music Club. She was not sure at this moment.

The job was finished. The feeling was that everybody had to look to the future. Gradually people faded away. Jack and Angela said their goodbyes; Liao and Chan had an emotional farewell with Angela; they were happy yet they were sad.

Liao quipped with levity, "Cheer up. It is not the end of the world. I have great confidence there will be another crime somewhere, sometime to investigate."

Jack responded, "When there is another situation, do not call us, we will call you."

They laughed as they walked out together to go their own ways; they did not know when they would see each other again.

Jack commented to Angela, "Let's get out of here and get home as quickly as we can."

Angela responded, "Aye, Captain."

EPILOGUE

The Country Music Club was never the same. It had become a popular place for the Chicago Police Department members to hang out. It now was one of the safest night clubs around; the local tough guys even complained to the owner about how many police were there; the owner smiled.

Bruno resumed his job as the bouncer with a smile on his face as he now had a much easier time of it with so many of the Chicago PD present.

Chief Investigator Liao and Assistant Investigator Chan returned to China to resume their campaign against wrong doers. They laughed a lot as they talked about the "sting" in Chicago.

Chief Detective Donald Matthews went back to investigating criminal activities. He was proud of his role in the "sting" operation.

Dr. Schmitt and Dr. Reidaman continued to make people "whole" as that was their special calling in life; they occasionally discussed how Angela's injuries turned out so well.

Wolfman was beside himself when he realized how the wool had been pulled over his eyes or how he had been duped.

Hogjowl had feelings of being watched as he conducted his nefarious activities. He was correct.

Mike Nussbaum returned to his passion of teaching but smiled when he thought of his role in this great deception.

The judge swelled with pride as he remembered his old friend's daughter and how she conducted herself with dignity and purpose.

Bradley Crawford returned to teaching, soon retired, and became a well-travelled international tourist.

The headmaster of Changsha Middle School placed "junior" in an institution that helped him. The teachers were relieved to be rid of him.

Uneventful days passed for Jack and Angela. Jack planted crops on his plantation and, as he often said, watched them grow from the porch on the house. On the porch it was possible to adjust the amount of wind off the Prairie by moving to another part of the porch. There was also the pond where they could paddle around in a little paddleboat, and they could fish off a fishing pier at one end of the pond. A wooden swing on the pond bank gave them an opportunity to sit and watch the sun set as the sun reflected off the pond water.

One day, Jack asked Angela if she missed her family, grandfather and grandmother.

"Of course," she replied. "Is that not true of everybody?"

"Yes, it is," said Jack, "Not a day goes by but what memories of my mother and father do not remind me of them. A person has to find their own place in the sun and to go forward. The past is but prologue to the future. We always start tomorrow."

One evening, there was a knocking at the door of the farmhouse. Jack opened the door and nearly swallowed his tongue, "You. It is you again."

"Yes," said Chief Investigator Liao, "I am here."

www.ingramcontent.com/pod-product-compliance
Lightning Source LLC
Chambersburg PA
CBHW031025190726
48286CB00003BA/1023